ADMISSIONS

ADMISSIONS

ADMISSIONS

*Tales of life, death & love
in a hospital not far from here ...*

Mira Harrison

ISBN 978-0-9951433-9-5 (Paperback)

BOOKS

Published by Copy Press Books, Nelson, New Zealand 2021
Copy Press Books, 141 Pascoe Street, Nelson, New Zealand

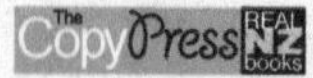

Distributed in New Zealand by CopyPress, Nelson, New Zealand.
www.copypress.co.nz

Contents

Author's note

The hospital in *Admissions* is fictional and any resemblance to actual healthcare facilities in any country is coincidental. While these stories are set in southern Aotearoa, where I now live and work, they are based on experiences training and working in public hospitals in the United Kingdom and New Zealand over many years. During my early career in medicine I undertook most of the jobs performed by the characters in *Admissions* and these tales are told from my perspective, rather than that of any other doctor or healthcare worker.

The characters in this book are also works of fiction. I created the eight women — and the other supporting roles — from my imagination, drawing on many different people I have met in healthcare institutions worldwide. There is an underlying reality to all these tales, but any resemblance to actual persons, living or dead, is coincidental.

Each tale may be read independently, but I encourage you to read them in the sequence presented. They have been curated with unifying themes and chronologies in mind — for example, starting with new beginnings and birth, moving through to the end of life and death. There are links between the characters which develop through the book, and I hope these will give you increased enjoyment as the tales progress.

Mira Harrison
September 2018

The Receptionist's Tale

~ RAELENE ~

About a year ago something happened that changed my outlook on life in a fundamental way. It occurred in the small city where I live, where I have always lived, and while the events took place in a dot on the map at the bottom of the globe, they brought the world to me.

Until the time when this story began, my life had been ordinary. I was born and raised in this town in the far south of Aotearoa, I went to school, passed my exams, then got a job at our local public hospital. Of course, there was much more to it than that — I argued with my parents when I was a teenager; I made friends, some of whom I kept, some I lost. And I fell in love with a guy in my year at high school. I say 'fell in love' but I now know it was lust, not love, and after too much lusting without the right precautions, the inevitable happened and I found I was pregnant. Confused and cornered, I married Steve in some haste and gave birth to Melissa a few months later. Her birth was easy enough, but the first weeks of parenting were a shock to two previously unencumbered and selfish young people, and after a few months, Steve left. He went back to drinking with his friends most nights of the week.

I carried on living in the cramped, dark flat we were renting, and looked after Melissa. Although it was hard being a solo mum, it was a relief when Steve left. His needs drained me as much as the baby I now found myself responsible for, and my needs didn't even feature in his world, so it was simpler when he wasn't there. It was calmer too — comforting a crying baby is easier than pacifying a dissatisfied and angry young man. The last time Steve hit me, I told him to leave and not come back. I adjusted to being on my own with Melissa quite quickly, but then we hadn't had much time with anyone else.

I went back to work when Melissa was nine months old. It wasn't because they desperately wanted me back, or that I was a crucial part of the Kiwi healthcare system: I was just a receptionist on the front desk of an average district hospital. I returned because I had to get out of my gloomy flat and escape the loneliness of being a single parent, at least for a few hours a week. The hospital daycare wasn't too expensive — and Melissa seemed happy enough there — so if I worked at least thirty hours a week, I could earn just enough money to keep my head above water. It wasn't only about getting out of the house and earning my own wages either — although I hated the idea of being on benefits — it was because I enjoyed my job. I still enjoy my job. I'm just a small part of an anonymous and pretty run-down establishment, but I am its front woman, its face if you like. Usually I'm the first person people meet on entering our hospital and I love that. Over the years, I must have met thousands of people: all the staff, patients and visitors who come through our front doors. I have known some for less than a few minutes and others, like my friend Rosie, for more than twenty years.

So I continued in the job I loved for all the years I was a young mum, seeing Melissa start school and progress through all the stages I'd done before her. Our life wasn't always easy — we had little support from family and money was tight, but I had a couple of close friends who kept me going when I thought I couldn't take it any more. As well as Rosie, who's a nurse up on Level 8, I had Gaylene, who used to work on the paediatric ward. She would joke about looking after kids all day and then going home to the little buggers every night too. We all put our kids in the hospital daycare, and having a chat and a smoke together was what kept us going in those days.

Melissa and I led a relatively simple life — work and school in the week, playgrounds and parks and sometimes the beach at the weekend. We didn't have holidays away from our town, but in summer I'd take a week off work and we would have what we called our special days, planning a whole day out, treating ourselves and doing things we really enjoyed doing together. That's my best memory of Melissa's childhood, and thoughts of those special days still make me smile, now she has grown up and gone.

After Melissa finished school and moved away, I carried on working at the hospital. I could do more hours and give it more energy now. You may think being a receptionist is pretty boring, that each day is more or less the same, that the effort required is fairly constant, but it's not how I've found it. No two days are the same at my desk. Of course, there are patterns — Tuesdays and Thursdays are coronary angiography days on Level 6, and gynae outpatients runs on Wednesdays on Level 1. There are many timetables and patterns in a hospital: when I'm training new receptionists I show them all the files, but I say you always have to check, because things change all the time. Receptionists have to be adaptable too — we are not always told when things change. I'm making it sound like rocket science I know, but there's more to it than you might think. Much of our work is meeting and greeting, giving directions and filling out forms, but there is a skill to what we do. Noticing things is part of our work.

It was during a new receptionist's training session that I first noticed Mohammed. I was in the middle of one of my motivational talks to Courtney, who had previously worked in an office doing IT support.

"Receptionists have to be 'people people'," I explained enthusiastically, although Courtney was already looking a bit bored.

"There's no point doing this job if you don't care about people," I was saying, when I became aware of a man waiting near our reception desk. I remember thinking immediately he didn't seem like a local — it wasn't just his dark skin, jet-black hair and neatly trimmed beard — it was his stance, his approach, or rather his lack of it. The men in our town stride up to reception desks and demand attention. This guy just waited patiently, seeking my invitation to approach, and I noticed that.

I looked over and smiled my receptionist's smile. "Good morning, morena." I added the Maori greeting — as encouraged in the training manual I helped write — but I was pretty sure he wasn't Maori. "Can I help you?"

He spoke politely, quietly, "Please, where I should report? I am here to work as a theatre porter. Today is my first day."

I smiled again and gave him instructions and a map of the hospital, modelling professional friendliness and efficiency in front of Courtney, who was hovering uncertainly behind me. When he had gone she said, "Well, he seemed like a strange one!"

I was going to pick her up on this, discuss her attitude, but as it was her first week I thought I'd leave it. It was only later that I thought I should have welcomed the stranger to our hospital, welcomed him to our town, introduced myself. Normally, I would have done all that, but in that brief moment when we first met, I was mesmerised by the sadness of his dark brown eyes. I also regretted not asking him where he was from. At first, I thought he might be from India, but I wasn't really sure.

During the following weeks I noticed the new porter took his lunch to the staff courtyard we have behind the Atrium, which is the fancy name some bigwig dreamt up for the hospital reception when they built this place back in the '70s. I like the courtyard, because on good days it's sunny and warm and on bad days — which are many in our far-flung southern land — it's at least sheltered from the winds which blast us, sometimes for weeks on end. The courtyard feels a world away from the main hospital and the Patients' Association has planted it up with some tree ferns and other native plants. But the walls are now cracked and mouldy, because no one has fixed a bit of broken guttering which leaks above our heads if we sit in the wrong spot.

Sometimes I take my lunch to the courtyard to see who I can catch up with. Gaylene doesn't work here any more and Rosie works nights, so it's often Rachel, whose kids are still young and tiring her out. They are great kids but, as I always say to her, even great kids are bloody exhausting.

One day I noticed him sitting alone at one of the wooden tables.

"Can I sit here?" I gestured towards the empty seats as I put my lunchbox down.

He smiled and nodded and only later — much later — he explained how strange it felt to him in those early days to be approached by a woman in this way: it was not what he was used to.

"I'm Raelene, from Reception. We met on your first day." I cheerfully introduced myself (I didn't forget this time) and then added, "How's it going?" in my friendliest Kiwi-speak.

"Hello Raelene, my name is Mohammed. It is good to meet you again," he replied, rather formally. We exchanged a few more pleasantries and I chatted away about the hospital, which I can talk about for hours, having worked here for so long. Mohammed listened and I talked some more, until I realised I was talking too much and should have at least asked him where he came from. When he told me he was from Syria, I was embarrassed as I didn't really know where that was. Of course I had heard about it on the news and knew there was a terrible war going on there, and I also knew that our city had recently accepted a group of Syrian refugees. The paper had featured articles about families being resettled and there had been photos of people growing vegetables and learning how to cook. I looked at Mohammed's lunchbox and wanted to ask him about all the colours and flavours and smells, but I really wanted to ask him if he was a refugee. Suddenly it all felt a bit intrusive, so I wrapped up the remains of my sandwich and said I had to get back to work.

That night I searched online for news articles about Syria, but there were so many it was confusing, and it left me feeling sad and bewildered. I changed my search to Syrian food and that was much better. I found photos of exotic dishes, some of which I recognised, because hummus has become quite popular. I learned that Syrian cooking is similar to Turkish cuisine, but that didn't help, because I wasn't really sure what they eat in Turkey either. Melissa knows about other countries and these new foods and she tells me they are not new, people have been eating them for hundreds of years. I'm embarrassed about my ignorance of foreign places.

The next day I asked Mohammed if he was a refugee and he said "sort of". That confused me again and for a moment I couldn't fill the silence with my usual chatter. He said that while he had not been part of the recent Syrian groups resettled in our town, he was indeed a refugee as he had left Syria after all his family had been killed. Now I really couldn't speak. What do you say when someone tells you that? We sat there in silence for an over-long moment and I was glad that most of the other staff had left. The courtyard was almost empty and I remember looking up into the fronds of the tree fern we were sitting under and thinking,

I live in one of the safest countries in the world, so how could I possibly understand that? I wanted to ask so many questions — who were his family? who did he lose? how could he possibly cope with their deaths? — but I just said "I'm really sorry, that's terrible."

I didn't see Mohammed for a few days after that. I wondered if he was working different shifts, as he didn't come through Reception during the hours I was working. In my job I get to know people's routines, when to expect them. He wasn't in the courtyard at lunchtime either and, even when I was chatting to Rachel or someone else, I found myself missing our conversations. He returned after a few days, explaining that he had been working nights. Mohammed was easy to talk to. He listened intently to everything I had to say and for several weeks we met regularly to eat our lunch. We never planned to meet, but it just happened that we were there at the same time. I nattered on about the hospital, the city, our country and, as he was newly arrived, he liked to "listen and learn" as he would put it. I told him things I thought a foreigner would need to know, what I thought our customs were, but then I found myself wondering if we really had many traditions and what they meant. It made me think about what it means to be from somewhere and I asked him if things were the same in Syria.

"In what way?" he asked.

"In any way. Just tell me anything you want to about where you're from — I know nothing about it."

As we talked, I came to appreciate that largely things were *not* the same in Syria, not in most ways. His stories were fascinating and sad and beautiful too — like his eyes, which I had noticed the first time we met. He never mentioned his family and I never talked about mine.

As summer moved on, a holiday weekend loomed and I decided I would ask Mohammed if he'd like to come on a day out with me. Usually I spent these days at home, tidying the house, perhaps a bit of gardening — nothing that interesting. I didn't know where he lived, but I pictured him alone in a cold flat, maybe cooking up lunches for the following week. So I suggested I take him on a day trip, a visit to a local beach, maybe a picnic.

"I could show you the sights," I enthused, adding that I could tell him more about the town where we lived.

"That would be wonderful." He seemed surprised but delighted by the invitation. "How will we travel?"

"I'll drive, of course." I guessed he probably didn't have a car. "And we don't want to have to catch the bus on a holiday weekend in this town."

He smiled when I said that and I noticed him looking at me directly. I wondered what was funny, because until then he was not someone who smiled much at all.

It turned out to be a lovely day. The weather in our part of the world is notoriously unreliable and as we drove out of town, I told Mohammed that some people call our coastline the Riviera of the Antarctic. He laughed and said he hadn't felt warm since leaving Syria, but it was very scenic here and that made up for the cold. He brought food — so much food — which we ate as a picnic on a small grassy area overlooking a rocky bay. I was amazed by how many dishes he had made and how delicious they all were, including one with eggplant, that mysterious purple vegetable I had seen in the supermarket, but had never known what to do with. When I told him this, he said that the Turks had at least one hundred and fifty ways of cooking aubergine and I felt pleased to know that Turkish cuisine is similar to Syrian cooking.

It was at this point I decided to tell him about Melissa, about my family, my life story, such as it was. It wasn't a tactic to learn about his family: I just wanted to tell him, I wanted him to know more about me. He had finished eating and lay down on his side on the grass to listen. It was the first time I had ever seen him relaxed, he was always so formal in his manners, but it made me feel more at ease. His dark eyes watched my face as I told my story. Occasionally his long lashes rested for a moment on his cheeks, then his eyes fixed on me again, held me there.

When I had finished, he was still looking at me — he had this way of being very still, quiet and calm. He said gently that he thought I was a strong woman. For some reason my eyes filled with tears and I suddenly felt vulnerable and young in his presence, although I knew I must be years older than him. I reached for my sunnies in an attempt to hide my tears, but somehow his hand was there instead and then he was holding my hand and stroking it gently. I was now crying uncontrollably and wanted to explain that this was not like me, I hadn't cried in years — it was generally me mopping up other people's tears, comforting the sick, sorting out the kids. But I couldn't speak at all. Then my head was on his chest and my tears were soaking his clean white cotton shirt. I felt his arms wrap around me and the side of his face against the top of my head. In that moment — the first that I'd been close to anyone for so long — Mohammed smelt like another world. We sat like that for some time, him holding me, stroking my back, his fingers running down along the line of my shoulder blade and up again to the nape of my neck, slowly, over and over again. I rested my head on his shoulder and he played with my hair as if he were exploring something for the first time. When I had stopped crying I could see the harbour glistening in the late summer sun.

That day was a turning point for us — the time at which our friendship became much closer. After my outpouring during our picnic we were quiet for a while, then we talked about this and that. Later that afternoon as we drove around the bays, Mohammed told me more about himself and his life before he came to our country. At one point I had to stop the car and ask him to repeat what he had just said, because I thought he had told me that in Syria he was a doctor.

"I was. I am!" He laughed at the way my mouth had dropped open as I pulled the car off the road. "I used to be a surgeon at a large hospital in Aleppo. Honestly. I am telling you the truth." He wasn't smiling now.

Once I had recovered from the shock and closed my mouth, I asked, "Do the other theatre staff know? Does anyone have any idea? What about Dr Malik?" I thought he might have confided in the lovely Indian anaesthetist all my friends had their eyes on.

"I haven't told anyone until now."

"Why not?" I was still incredulous.

He explained that his qualifications were not recognised in our country and despite his repeated attempts, the New Zealand Medical Council would not register him. After several months, he had needed work — any work — and a theatre porter was the closest he could find to what he did at home. I was aghast: I started babbling that he must have trained for so long, must have so much experience in trauma surgery, that he should tell everyone who he is, what he can do, what he *could* do if they just let him.

"They should let you do some of the more difficult cases. Or you could teach our trainee doctors how to do surgery." From what I'd heard, some of them needed help.

Mohammed laughed again. "It doesn't quite work like that. Rules are rules and have to be followed."

I was glad he could laugh about it, but I couldn't understand how he could go to work each day and see others do the operations he was so qualified to perform. I started thinking about what I could find out, who I could ask, as I knew there was a shortage of surgeons in our region. Surely doing the work he was qualified for would help him heal, would relieve the sadness in his eyes?

* * *

A year later and my world has changed so much since I met Mohammed. After our day trip we went out together a few more times as friends. Mohammed has always been proper about our relationship and things developed, although not in a physical way. Sometimes we held hands, but no more than that, until the day he asked me to become his wife. We were again out beside the harbour and again my mouth dropped open and we both started laughing. By then I'd told him I was in my fifties (although I was a bit vague about which end of the decade I fell into) and knew he was more than ten years younger than me, so of course I had to say no.

"You should find a younger woman, so you could have children and become a dad and then you could all live happily ever after in our Land of the Long White Cloud." I wanted him to have all the happiness he was deprived of in Syria.

"I don't want a younger woman. I want you, Raelene."

I didn't respond — I was still in shock.

"What does age matter if you love someone?" Mohammed asked.

I couldn't argue with that, and we continued walking hand in hand on a grassy footpath above the sea. When we found a bench to sit on, I told him I had loved him since the day he took me in his arms on our first picnic, knowing it was such a cliché, but I had to be truthful with him. Sharing our truths had brought us together: we had shared our pasts, our stories, now with a common ending. I found myself in a man from the other side of the world, and what was once so foreign is now so familiar.

It's not just a dreamy romance either — I've helped him reapply to the Medical Council (after he finally asked Anil how to go about this) and he is now 'retraining under supervision', as the Council call it, although I bet Mohammed will teach them a few things. One of the gynae profs was great too — we were chatting when she came down to Reception to tell me that there'd been some changes to her day surgery list. The idiots who protest outside our hospital every week were causing more problems than usual. She told me she thought the orthopaedic lot could really do with some help from an experienced trauma surgeon. A couple of weeks later, Mohammed got a letter saying they would be pleased to supervise him.

We don't live together yet (I told you he was proper) but Mohammed has met Melissa and it's all going surprisingly well. I was worried because it had been Melissa and me for so long, but they got on from the start and they've even shared a few recipes. She cried like a baby when we told her we were officially engaged to be married, but she was laughing at the same time, so I thought she must be happy about it and told her not to be so soft.

The news has caused quite a stir at the hospital too. Rosie and Rachel were both over the moon for me, but Courtney couldn't believe it. I watched her run off to tell anyone she could find to tell, leaving me holding the fort as usual. For days after that I could sense people whispering about us in the courtyard, in the canteen, on the different paths throughout our workplace. When I saw Rosie at the end of her shift one morning, she said the night porters had been chatting about Mohammed and me. Normally, I try not to get involved in hospital gossip, but I have to admit, I've quite enjoyed hearing the story of the receptionist and the refugee repeated with varying degrees of truthfulness.

~

The Obstetrician's Tale

Labour Ward is like a war zone today. It's one of those days. If tanks suddenly crashed through the double doors under the sign 'Delivery Suite', none of us who work here would be surprised — or if we were, we wouldn't show it. I'm the most senior doctor on Labour Ward today: the obstetric registrar on call, and I still use the old name for my unit long after the hospital managers renamed it during one of their *Progressing Change* exercises. Apparently, Delivery Suite sounds more professional. Perhaps they also thought it would disguise the agony of what goes on here to those outside our doors. I bet no one on their working group had delivered a baby, or been in labour themselves. It would be nice to think that mothers were in some way involved in the rechristening of our unit, but I'm pretty sure no one asked them.

One of my first teachers in obstetrics — an ancient, well-fed Irish gentleman who had been attending women in labour forever, and always did so wearing a three-piece suit whatever the time of night or day — used to say, "Labour is called labour because it's *hard work*. There's no getting away from it, and in time, those of you who attend women in labour, or indeed labour yourselves, will see that I am right."

Both in the classroom and at the bedside, he went on to teach us the importance of the active management of labour. Mr Rawlinson was a wonderful teacher, old-fashioned in his manners and ways, but spot-on in his clinical judgment and surgical technique. I learned so much from him — how to deliver breech babies, babies facing the wrong way, too-small babies, too-large babies and all the other babies who couldn't find their way out into the world without assistance. He taught me how to operate with precision and to intervene only when needed, but hardest of all, how to stay calm in the face of any obstetric crisis.

As his juniors, we felt his reassuring presence and he was always there for us, even at 3 a.m., immaculate in his suit and tie. Underneath his grand old gent appearance, Mr Rawlinson was unfailingly respectful and kind to everyone, especially women in labour. He would sometimes place his hand on their shoulder, or arm or foot (depending on his position relative to them) when he was explaining a procedure. He was a master of his craft and we were all shocked when he announced his retirement last year. As was his way, he told us himself, before the official memo went around. A small group of us were in the Labour Ward tearoom, including Anil, one of the anaesthetists, and Sarah, our new Prof, who Mr Rawlinson himself had trained. He was gracious and dignified, saying it was time to hand on the baton — or rather the forceps — and that he knew Sarah would be marvellous. As we sipped our tea, we tried not to show we were stunned he was leaving us.

Anil managed to ask some polite questions about his plans for retirement, but my eyes filled with tears, my heart with dread. No one tried to persuade him otherwise. He knew it was time and we respected that.

* * *

As I said, today is busy on Labour Ward. We have eight thousand deliveries a year, an average of twenty-two births every twenty-four hours. You might estimate that to be about one baby born each hour, but obstetrics is never so predictable. We can plan for some births — I've done two elective sections today — but most of our work is completely random. This morning I've also done an emergency section, a rotational forceps delivery, two more straightforward forceps deliveries and a Ventouse delivery, where we use a suction cap on the baby's head to vacuum it into the world. And it's not yet lunchtime.

Julie, one of the senior midwives on L2, the antenatal ward, just phoned me.

"Hi Mary, I hear it's chaos down there today."

"Only the usual chaos. What's up?" I tried to sound casual.

"I have a multip with twins who'll need to come down before too long. She was booked for a section tomorrow, but she's contracting. Sorry!"

"No worries. Membranes intact?" I tried to sound calm.

"At the moment."

We both knew it wouldn't be long.

"History?"

"Two normal deliveries. The last one in four hours." Julie sounded stressed.

"Okay, we just need to find a room. And hopefully an anaesthetist. I'll get back to you."

This is not unusual. I've been an obstetric registrar for about six months now, so although I'm not very experienced, I'm learning fast. I enjoy the pace, the action, the fact it's never boring. It's terrifying, but also exhilarating to bring new life into this world, and I like the surgical procedures too. As a med student, I got the highest grades in our year in the surgical attachments, although it wasn't until later that I really got to do anything. Now, I'm finding my way. I always pause — the smallest imperceptible pause — when I'm fully scrubbed and ready to start: breathe in, breathe out. Even in an emergency there is time to prepare. Mr Rawlinson taught us to always have everything ready — instruments, fluids, drugs — to set them all out neatly on the steel trolleys where you can find your tools easily. And most importantly, to *think* first. "Preparation is all!" he used to say and Anil would joke that Rawly must have been a boy scout back in the day. Anil is great, always knows what to say. I've learned the value of anaesthetists who can chat, because our patients are almost always awake — often with supporters at their side — and there's an art to carrying on a conversation during an obstetric emergency. I'm getting better at it, but sometimes there isn't time for niceties, we just have to get the baby out.

Once you start, the adrenaline rushes as the first cut is made, or the first blade of the forceps is placed around the baby's head, or as your hand reaches in for that tiny foot. After that, there's no time to think until the infant screams its first breath and the bleeding is under control, which might take a while. There's a lot of blood in our job and it's hard to measure the amount in deliveries, because it's all mixed up with amniotic fluid on the theatre floor and splashing down our aprons and soaking into our scrubs. Our battles are bloody and adrenaline helps us through them, but our bodies' chemicals are a quick fix and the high doesn't last long, before tiredness sets in. Mr Rawlinson used to say there are two lives in our hands, sometimes more, and the obstetrician does not rest until the mother is safe. Delivering requires stamina from the obstetrician as well as from the labouring woman. It's hard work all round.

* * *

This hospital has been my life for years. That makes me sound old — I've just turned twenty-eight and I've been a doctor for four years. I was a student here too and it's become my second home — or maybe my first, as I spend more time here than at our house these days. I did leave for a few months to do some postings at district hospitals. My first time outside a teaching hospital was quite an experience — at one remote clinic, the nurses tried to book me in and weigh me, until I persuaded them I wasn't a patient, but the doctor. I've always looked young, I guess (although I'm not short or slight) and perhaps being called Mary suggested a more motherly than medical role to those nurses out in the wop-wops.

I'm from the sticks myself: I was born and raised on a small island far away in a large ocean. It's a long way from anywhere — several flights from here — hours and hours of travel. My home is a remote atoll which hasn't much more than a lot of coconut palms and fish to make a living from. Photos of our white sand beaches sometimes feature in glossy magazines — our government is desperately encouraging tourism — but it's not the tropical paradise you might imagine. Not to live there anyway. It is beautiful, though. Especially the turquoise lagoon where we swam as kids.

My mother gave birth to me in our hospital, which sits on a hill overlooking the sea. It's one of those buildings that was put up hastily in the Second World War, but has lasted reasonably well and has a shady garden where new mothers can cradle their babies and look out over the ocean beyond. Mum tells me I was a big baby, but I came into this world easily. She also says I was a determined child, that I always knew where I was going. There's no university in our country and many of us even attend high school in places far from home. It was hard to leave to be educated in cold and alien lands, but Aotearoa has been good to me and I've got used to the frosts and snow of South Island winters. I would even say I like it: it's a different kind of beauty.

Kiwi friends sometimes ask me if my islands are a quiet place to live and I laugh and say, "No way! There's always noise — cockerels crowing, pigs squealing and my aunties yelling. The politicians make a big racket too."

I might also tell them that, even when you think it's quiet, there's the continual low thunder of the waves crashing onto the reef that protects our land. We kids were told *never* to go beyond the reef on our own. I wasn't tempted to — the sea on the other side sounded angry to me. Part of my prayers included thanks for the guardianship of those rocks that allowed us to play safely in our lagoon. One of my friends suggested that maybe there was a taniwha protecting us too. It would be a long way from home, but apparently taniwha are good swimmers.

I went back to my island for a few weeks to do a student elective in the hospital where I was born. I enjoyed going home, even with my parents continually showing me off at church and at dinners for family and friends. We have a large family, English on one side (my father's) and our gatherings are chaotic — despite Dad's attempts at organising everyone — and loud. There's a lot of music-making when we get together and there are so many of us, we could form a choir — except we don't need to, as everyone is in the church choir. During that visit, when I was a med student, my grandparents (on Mum's side) kept telling me the story of our island's most famous doctor who, like me, trained in New Zealand. He returned home with his Kiwi wife, to look after his people for many years. Later, he went on to become involved in politics, but in doing that he stopped being our doctor and someone else took his place. Now I can see that, like Mr Rawlinson, he had to move on.

* * *

Today I don't seem to have as much stamina and energy as usual. There is something going on in my body which I am trying to hide from my colleagues on Labour Ward. Four weeks ago, I discovered I am pregnant. It came as a bit of a shock, although Joe and I have been married for three years, and a few months ago we had a vague discussion about having children. It was late at night, we had both been working many hours that week — Joe's a doctor too, a GP registrar — and we were seeking solace in each other (and in a bottle of red wine, but don't tell my parents) so I can't quite remember how it went. I don't think we agreed anything specific, but I stopped taking my pill and when my period didn't arrive, I went to a pharmacy to buy a pregnancy test. I made sure to go to a chemist on the other side of town from the hospital, rather than nick one from the ward. With pregnancy test in brown paper bag, stuffed deep into my handbag clutched high under my right arm, next to my tender, swollen breasts, I scuttled to the car and drove home wearing my dark glasses. I remember every set of traffic lights went against me on that journey and I wondered if it was a sign.

When Joe got home later I said, "I've done it." He looked at me, but I gave nothing away. I didn't know what to say, how to tell him. I thought about the movies we had seen together, where the lovely young mother-to-be glows as she tells her husband, "Darling, I'm having your baby," but I just felt physically sick. Fear ran through my body.

Eventually I stuttered "Yep," and Joe smiled, a bit anxiously. I wondered why I didn't feel happy. Wasn't this what we wanted?

The week after the test was very busy at work and I felt lousy. Nauseated and bloated, I sat at the Labour Ward station writing up my notes. None of the other staff noticed the sign I was sure was stamped on my forehead saying "PREGNANT!", or if they did notice, they didn't say. Our work went on as usual — erratically stressful and exhausting as ever.

One morning in the antenatal clinic, as I scanned and palpated, I tried asking other mothers-in-waiting how they felt when they first discovered they were pregnant. No one said they were delighted. The most helpful comment came from a woman having her sixth baby, who said it was good job pregnancy was nine months long, because it takes that much time to get used to the idea. I could not imagine going through *this* six times. Women who have had lots of babies are called Grand Multips in obstetrics. We have a deliberately mysterious language, which includes how we notate the number of pregnancies and births each woman has had. For example, I would be labelled 'Gravida 1, Para 0' or 'primiparous" (primip for short) because I'm pregnant for the first time, but I've not yet delivered. Or I would have been labelled like this, if I had told any of my colleagues I was pregnant.

Three more weeks passed and I thought I might phone my sister to confide in her — she's had two children (both born at home with no obstetric intervention required) and doesn't hold back when it comes to talking about childbirth. She once told a whole family gathering that having a baby was like shitting a football, which didn't go down well with my parents, whose devout beliefs include not talking about any parts of our bodily systems. But I didn't get time to phone her and then last week I started bleeding. It was just some spotting at first and Joe was calm and reassuring, reminding me it was common in the early weeks and that everything would be okay. Sensible Joe, the GP-in-waiting. My experience as an obstetrician had taught me that everything was *not* always okay, but I didn't argue.

I carried on at work as if nothing was wrong. In some ways, on-call days on Labour Ward were the easiest to get through because I had less time to worry, less time to visit the toilet and check my pad for more blood, or fresh blood, or whatever might come next. It stopped and it started again. Joe suggested I take a day off to put my feet up, but there was no one to cover for me. He asked if I wanted to see my GP, but I didn't want to, as my doctor works at Joe's practice and someone would be sure to see me in the waiting room. I wanted to keep this private for now. So I fought my own battle with the bleeding. I willed it to stop, I prayed for it to stop so that my baby would have a chance.

It didn't stop and today it is worse. There was fresh blood on my pad when I went to the toilet between each procedure this morning. Bright red blood soaking through the layers of my sanitary protection. I should call Joe, but I can't, for so many reasons. This afternoon I'm having cramps, which feel like period pains, except they are now coming every few minutes in waves, like contractions. I am starting to labour and I don't know what to do. I know I should know — I've been trained — but now this is me, I can't think straight. Thankfully the ward is still busy, so I can hide my anxiety by going from room to room to check on all the other labouring women. In one room, I need to stay and do a lift-out forceps, in another I have to repair an episiotomy. I'm just hoping there won't be anything too physically demanding — at least I can sit down to stitch a perineum.

Later on, I have to call one of the consultants about the twins. Labour is going well and I managed to find the on-call anaesthetist — not Anil today, but Dave's fine, if not so chatty. The first babe is cephalic presentation (head first, good news) and Mum is still smiling, although she won't be for long. Women stop smiling at full dilatation. I can't get hold of my boss, as he's at the private hospital on the other side of town. We call it the Poshpital as it's so shiny and new — and only offers its services to the well off or well insured — but it's no joke that the newer, younger consultants spend so much of their time down the road, earning the cash they need to pay off the loans on their brand-new BMWs. Mr Rawlinson would never have done it.

I decide I am going to have to make my own plan for the twins, but I'll need to find another pair of hands to help me, especially if we are going for a vaginal delivery, which we are. Mr Rawlinson taught me the vaginal route is usually best (he was scathing of the modern trend to perform a section on almost everyone), but *never* to attempt to deliver twins on your own. So I need help and I won't get it from my consultant this time. I wish Sarah was around, but she's away at a conference this week. The midwives will play their part and I'm sure the Senior House Officer will step in, but she has never delivered twins vaginally before. I'll have to give her careful instructions while doing my own job at the same time. I hope I can do it.

My pains continue into the early evening and I can feel the bleeding becoming heavier. I'm hoping it won't soak through my scrubs as I make my way to the toilet again. We have just delivered the twins ("a wee boy and a wee girl!" as the midwives like to announce) and although everything went to plan, it was hard to concentrate as my cramps were becoming more intense. The first twin was a normal delivery, so I let the SHO handle that, as I palpated the second twin to determine position. After the epidural had been topped up, I was able to move twin two into cephalic presentation and after a bit more time and an excellent effort from Mum, I brought him out with Neville Barnes forceps. The wee boy cried loudly and the new mother smiled again. The paeds swooped in to take the babes and the room became crowded and noisy, as it always is for twins. I delivered the placenta, checked the bleeding, then had to leave.

Now I go to the doctors' changing room at the end of the corridor. Someone at the desk is calling my name and another woman is being wheeled through our double doors, surrounded by an entourage of family and friends, her labouring whanau. I keep walking, but when I get inside the toilet cubicle I'm brought to my knees by the pains. There is blood running down my legs as I kneel on the floor and I'm not sure whether to try and get up onto the toilet or stay where I am. I now know that this is the end of my pregnancy — but I can't miscarry into the toilet. I try to breathe, I try to prepare. I remove my scrubs, my pants, my pad, all soaked with blood that is starting to clot. There are pieces of tissue in the blood which is now weeping onto the white tiled floor and edging towards the door. Sitting in a pool of my own blood, all I can think of is that at home, we do not flush our babies down the toilet. We bury our dead in our front gardens, under sheltering trees.

In the end, it is not too bad. I am glad to be alone, as Joe would be too upset. I will tell him later and he will still be distraught, but just for now I can't cope with the grief of others. The intense pains have stopped. There is a stillness that follows labour, there is time to rest. I remain on the toilet floor and study the mess around me. Among the blood clots there is the smallest, smallest baby — we would call it a fetus of approximately ten weeks gestation, not a baby. But it is *my* baby and it has the tiniest hand I have ever seen. I study how delicate it is, how perfectly formed.

One of the cleaners is singing in the distance, in one of the Labour Ward toilets. I examine the pattern of the tiles, now stained with my blood and with my baby's blood. I've noticed the same off-white tiles everywhere: in theatre, on the wards, even in the canteen. This thought makes me realise I haven't eaten anything today, but it doesn't matter. The tiles are cracked and need re-grouting: this hospital is falling apart, no matter how hard we work to keep it going. I think about Mr Rawlinson. It's not likely that my new consultant will find me here in the middle of my own obstetric calamity and I'm glad about that. The new men of O&G are not kind and they don't understand what women go through to bring life into this world. Or sometimes not to bring life and to lose a part of yourself.

I should get up, but I can't seem to move. I am lying curled on my side on the floor and there is blood in my hair, although I am quite comfortable. My baby lies next to me and it is not yet time to say goodbye. I wish we were far away on our island, lying in a clean bed in a ward of the hospital on the hill. I could walk out into the garden and show my baby the large ocean beyond. We will go back there soon. Joe and I will go and we will take the remains of our tiny baby to bury there, in my parents' front garden.

I already know this is not my time to bring new life into this world. There will be other babies and other lives. Some of them I will bring into the world, surrounded by others who will welcome their entry under bright theatre lights as I pull and lift, using all the training and skill I can muster. Mr Rawlinson has gone, but he stays with me as I work through my days and nights, labouring on Labour Ward. He couldn't have helped me this time anyway. This time, my body failed me.

Joe will comfort me and tell me we are still young, and he is right. He will tell me there is hope and he is right about that too. He'll tell me that I *will* become a mother one day, but he won't be quite right about that. I became a mother today.

The Cleaner's Tale

~ RACHEL ~

I. *Moderato*

Every day I drive to work with music playing. Sometimes I let the kids listen to something they like, but mostly I impose my choice on them and play it loudly, so I can't hear them whinging beneath it. I know this sounds cruel, but if you have young children you'll know that all other parts of the day — and often the night — are spent following their routines and meeting their needs. Having any time to ourselves is but a distant memory, so my music in the car is just a small statement that there are fragments of my life left in these family-dominated days.

I love classical music. I've always loved it, even as a turbulent teenager. When I shaved half my head and became a Goth (I wore nothing but black for years) I got a treble clef tattooed on my back — high up, between my shoulder blades at the base of my neck. I also thought about getting musical notes tattooed down my arms, but to be honest, the treble clef was so painful, I left it at that. My friends didn't understand that I liked all sorts of music. For them, you were in one camp or the other. Me, I loved it all: orchestras, operas, new wave, punk rock, glam-rock, rock-opera — anything with music. I started learning the piano when I was three: my mother was musical and taught me as I sat on her knee. When I was older, she told me she had wanted to become a concert pianist, but her family couldn't afford to support her, so she'd had to go and work in an office until she married my father. After that, she gave up on any plans for a career in music, or anything else. She also told me she found being a mother of small children boring and frustrating, and the only way she could cope was with her music. Mum always said things like that — she was very dramatic.

On the way to school in the mornings I play an upbeat but not too hectic piece. One of my favourites is Rachmaninov's 'Rhapsody on a Theme of Paganini': it is *energico*! It's a rush to get out of the house after getting the kids up and dressed, making breakfasts, packing lunches and writing last-minute notes for their teachers. There's always some form to be filled in with instructions to RETURN THE PERMISSION SLIP IMMEDIATELY! We mothers are permission-granters on a daily basis, yet somehow I never feel quite in control of what I am permitting, especially in their school-world.

Sustaining the morning momentum, I get the kids into the car and fight my way through the traffic. 'Sustain' was my piano teacher's favourite word. Rachmaninov is my favourite composer (if I had to choose only one) and his Rhapsody is definitely morning music. I might also choose the first movement of his second piano concerto, as it's very rousing — and lasts just the right amount of time to get from home to Jacob's kindy.

When we get there, Katie likes to come in with us to deliver her little brother. She gives him instructions for the day in a loud operatic voice, saying things like, "Make sure you play with all the blocks today, Jacob!"

Katie used to attend this preschool before she started real school and she greets the staff as if she were a member of visiting royalty. She wafts in, inspects which toys are out for the little ones to play with and says, "Hello Gaylene, how are you today?"

"I'm well thanks, Katie," Gaylene replies with a grace I could not muster for an overly-superior six-year-old. Katie is much like her grandmother. On one occasion, she asked the kindy staff to call her Katarina, rather than boring old Katie. I find it all a bit embarrassing, but they seem to love her and it helps Jacob settle for the day. As we leave, he waves back at us with his chubby little hand.

There were times when it was not so easy leaving Jacob. When I first got my job at the hospital I hadn't left him in anyone else's care before, and he would scream his protest, his face red and blotchy with rage, his fingers clinging onto my legs as I tried to leave him. I'd been at home with the kids for five years, because that was what was expected of me. It was never discussed, and how could I raise it? Grant earned more than I did, and I was their mother. I had no other role and no choice — in our world mums stay at home with the babies and dads go out to work. Until I could take it no longer, that is. The loneliness was killing me. The exhaustion was killing me. The boredom was killing me and the number of cigarettes I smoked every day was probably killing me too.

Sometimes I'd get angry. Sometimes Grant came home from work late (I suspected he was deliberately missing happy hour, the feeding and bathing time before bed when babies scream loudest) and I was so angry I wanted to hit him. Sometimes I did hit him and then I ran to the bathroom and cried and smoked until I felt I should come out and make his dinner. As I watched him eat, my face still wet with tears, I said I couldn't take it any longer.

He didn't understand — he'd never spent a whole day on his own with pre-schoolers, had never struggled to the supermarket with two infants in tow, carrying them and all the groceries back home on the bus, to clean up the huge mess there wasn't time to deal with earlier. Grant hadn't taken a single day off work when the kids were born — he said mechanics didn't get paternity leave — and he went on as if nothing was different in his life. Nothing was that different for him after we had kids: I still cleaned his house, shopped for his food, made his meals and did his laundry. One of our worst fights was about his dirty socks and underpants, which he just dropped on the floor at the end of the day, expecting them to magically appear sometime later, clean and dry in his drawers, ready for the next use. Which they did, because I couldn't stand the mess around me all day at home. I was a good washerwoman, a good housekeeper — and I wanted to be a good wife and mother, but I couldn't do it because I was too angry.

After too many evenings of me crying on the doorstep as he came home from work, too many nights sleeping on the couch (we hadn't made love since before Jacob was born) and too many weekends when I begged him not to go and play football all day, he agreed I could try to find a job — so long as it paid more than daycare would cost. So I did. My work at the hospital isn't well paid — I'm only a cleaner after all — but it's enough to cover Jacob's kindy and now that Katie is at school, we can make ends meet. And it means I am not going mad any more.

Next stop in the morning is school, where the parking is a nightmare and I can feel my blood boiling as I negotiate the traffic and the other parents (some of them are very aggressive drivers) and try to find somewhere to stop for long enough to take Katie in. She loves school — she marches in — and likes me to follow to say our goodbyes in the playground, in front of the other children. This means in front of some of the parents too, and she looks up at me, waiting for me to say to her, "Make sure you do lots of reading today!" Or perhaps, "Make sure you win the races against the other kids!" But I'm not this type of mother, so I just say, "Have fun and I'll see you later," then rush back to the car, hoping no one has put a big dent in it.

Back on my journey, I might change the music if I've had to play something dreadful to get the kids to school. Or I'll continue with my own music, perhaps singing along, if it's an opera I'm listening to. I love opera. My favourite is *Eugene Onegin* by Tchaikovsky and the story is suitably tragic. It's all about loving people at the wrong time. I've never seen an opera performed live, but maybe one day one of those travelling companies will make it to our town.

By the time I get to work I'm usually less frazzled than when I left home, although that depends if I can park not too far away from the hospital. We all used to have free parks — even us cleaners — but then the management decided to sell the car park to a pharma company to build an Excellent Research Centre, whatever that is. So we now have to park on a road nearby (or not) and feed our wages into meters before walking the rest of the way to work.

As I come into the hospital, Raelene calls out, "Morning, Rachel!" and if she isn't too busy, I stop for a quick chat. She's a good sort — always asks about the kids, and at Easter and Christmas she buys them little presents. The kids love Raelene. Katie sometimes asks if she can come to work with me so she can sing Raelene one of her favourite songs. I tell her we don't have time for singing at work, although that's not quite true.

II. *Adagio sostenuto*

I am a cleaner in the mental health unit, but sometimes I work on other wards too. The psychiatric ward is not called this — all the wards have meaningless names like A1 or B4. It's like this throughout the hospital: only units like Delivery Suite or A&E give any hint to what goes on where — and if you don't work here, I don't know how you would know, unless you asked Raelene, who knows everything. I'm pretty sure the managers want it kept like this — they don't want people to know there are people having mental breakdowns in their hospital.

My day starts by helping with the breakfasts, clearing up after the patients have eaten at the communal table in the middle of the ward. Cleaners are not allowed to prepare or serve any food (Health and Safety Regulation 116.3 or some other directive) and the nurses don't really like us talking to the patients either. Cleaners are expected to be invisible in a hospital: it's a bit like Grant and his underpants — somehow the washing and the cleaning should just get done by somebody, and the nurses are glad that somebody isn't them.

Patients are encouraged to get up for breakfast and leave their bedrooms to join the others at the table, which is covered with a red and white checked cloth. It's meant to look cheerful and homely, but we all know that Ward B4 is neither of these things. The staff call it the Acute Psychiatric Ward, because it's where patients are put after a mental health crisis, like taking an overdose (common) or a first psychotic episode (not so common). There is a lot of waiting on B4. There are those waiting to see a psychiatrist, or just waiting to see what will happen next. Sometimes a doctor comes to see a patient, or a few of them go off for a group therapy session in a seminar room, but most of the time they just wait.

I'm not meant to know as much as I do about being a patient on Ward B4, but I was an inmate here once myself. It was years ago and most of the staff who work here now have no idea — or I hope they don't. I know that Sally, one of the psych nurses, looks up people's records using their personal details — and I don't mean just patients' records — so it's possible she knows about me. People think that hospital staff are so hard-working and honest, but I could tell you a few things.

I was admitted here when I was sixteen, after my mother committed suicide. I told you she was a drama queen. It was very unexpected — to me anyway — and I came home from school to find her. My dad was out at work and my younger sisters were at a birthday party somewhere else in town. Mum must have planned it all carefully and I still can't forgive her for arranging for it to be me who found her. I don't remember what I did in those first moments when I saw my mother was dead, but I do remember that the house was quiet — silent even — which was strange, as usually there was music. Not always happy music: sometimes Mum would be listening to something really sad (like the second movement of Rachmaninov's piano concerto in C minor), but there was always music. She rarely played herself in those days, because she had given away the upright piano she had when we were small — Mum said it was a crappy old thing and that when *she* played, it had to be on a decent instrument. My mother had wanted a baby grand, but Dad said we couldn't afford it on his wages, especially if we wanted anything else, like a holiday in the summer.

It wasn't until after the funeral that I lost the plot. Mum had written a long letter detailing her preferred funeral arrangements, which included a full performance of Mozart's Requiem Mass. Dad went mad in those terrible days following her death, saying he had no idea how to arrange a choir and orchestra to play at short notice and that he couldn't afford it anyway. During the psychotherapy I had later, the analyst — a strange long-haired hippie-type far too old to wear his hair in a ponytail — suggested that my father had never been able to give my mother what she wanted (not even after death) and this is what had made her so miserable. At the time this explanation seemed reasonable — and it helped alleviate some of the guilt I felt about her death — but once my brain was functional again I told the hippie-analyst that women shouldn't depend on men for happiness. He nodded thoughtfully and said I could start reducing my meds.

In the end, we held Mum's funeral in the red brick building where most people in our town seem to end up. It's called a funeral home (although no one lives there) and has a large room which would once have been called a chapel, but can be adapted to suit any religion — or no religion, like us. I remember wishing we were believers, because we could have had a proper funeral in an old church where the acoustics would have been wonderful for a full requiem mass, like Mozart's perfect composition. But my mother did not believe in heaven or hell and her final moments on earth were marked by a dry speech from a celebrant recommended by the funeral director. Neither of them had ever met Mum, who would have been disappointed by the lack of ceremony or drama in the service. I like to think I saved the day for her: the funeral parlour had a piano — it was a baby grand — and I played the solo part of the second movement of her favourite Rachmaninov concerto, so she got something of what she wanted.

I was a pretty good pianist in those days — I'd had lessons at school for years and didn't mind practising on the crappy uprights in the music department. I played Rachmaninov's saddest movement of his most passionate concerto, unaccompanied in that soulless room to the small gathering at my mother's funeral. It was a grey day, with rain looming, but shafts of sunlight briefly penetrated the windows as I made my way to the piano. I sat with my back to my family, who were in the front row. I could feel their eyes on me, on my treble clef tattoo, just above the neckline of my simple black dress. For a long moment I waited: to commune with Rachmaninov and hear the silence. My music teacher used to say the absence of notes, the pauses in music, were as important as the notes themselves. Raising my hands above the keys, my feet poised above the pedals, I entered the kingdom of music and played for Mum. As the last notes fell away from the final chord, I could hear my siblings crying.

* * *

Later, during the long hours of waiting on Ward B4, I learned more about Rachmaninov from another patient, a music teacher called Carl who had schizophrenia. Carl had been on B4 for weeks and rarely had any visitors: he spent most of his days on a couch in the day area, staring out of the window that looked onto the staff courtyard below. I don't know why he decided to talk to me, as he never chatted to anyone else. He told me that the C Minor piano concerto was first performed in 1901 with the composer as soloist. I tried to imagine Rachmaninov all that time ago, sitting at a huge grand piano as the lights in the concert hall dimmed and he raised his huge hands to play those first dramatic notes of his own concerto. But it was hard to concentrate in those B4 days. Trying to think about music exhausted me. After my performance at Mum's funeral I knew I would never play again.

The psychiatrists I saw when I was on the ward were not forthcoming with information about my condition. They were strange men and, to begin with, I didn't know they were doctors. Wandering over to me at random times of day, they would say things like,

"Hi, I'm Ted. How are you feeling today?"

I never knew how to answer that question. I didn't really feel anything, just emptiness. I suppose I could have told them I felt empty, but I didn't. I chose not to talk. I also chose not to play or sing, and I didn't go back to the kingdom for a long time. I overheard one of the strange men telling my dad I had suffered an episode of psychotic depression. I didn't feel especially sad as I sat looking at the walls for hours on end. I thought about Mum quite a lot, sometimes trying to picture her dead face as it stared up at me from the kitchen floor where we waited for Dad to come home. Her eyes had been open, I remembered that, and I had closed them.

I wondered whether I was like Mum, whether her actions had cemented my fate. I was like her now, sitting in a loony bin trapped by my depression and unable to escape. Would I be unable to find happiness, enjoy a fulfilling career, fall in love or follow another dream? Be unable to become a good, or even just adequate, mother? Even if I came through this now, would I become like Mum in years to come? Would there ever be any joy in my life?

I thought back to when I was six and first realised what it meant to die. Mum had been washing up in the kitchen and I was trying to help her. As she washed and I dried, I had asked her about death.

"What happens after we die, Mum?"

"Nothing happens," she said. "That's it. The lights go out and we are no more."

It terrified me. What a thing to say to a six-year-old! But maybe she was right to tell me the truth. She generally did. Since that moment in the kitchen, I've been frightened of death and of dying, and when the strange men were interviewing me on B4, I told them I was not going to kill myself. Even in those dim and silent days I knew that would be a pointless and stupid thing to do.

During another long afternoon on B4, when we sat like morons on the hospital couches, Carl told me that Rachmaninov dedicated his second piano concerto to his psychiatrist, Dr Nikolai Dahl, under whom he had completed a course of treatment. I tried to ask what had happened to the musical genius once my hero, but Carl was vague on the details of Rachmaninov's diagnosis or what caused it. I wasn't sure whether to believe anything he said anyway, because in those days I thought that people with schizophrenia were mad. (The boys at school used to shout "Schizo!" at anyone they thought was crazy.) There were some very odd people on our ward too. There was this woman who told me she was the Queen's illegitimate sister and had been sent to the other side of the world to be kept out of sight from British society. She'd spent most of her life writing letters to governments and ambassadors — and anyone else she could think of — who might help her. No one ever believed her, but I did.

It was almost Christmas when I was discharged from B4. The worst seemed to be behind me. I was still on large doses of mind-numbing meds, but the psychiatrists thought it would be okay for me to be numb at home. As I waited for Dad to come and pick me up one evening after he had finished work, I could hear singing somewhere in the distance. For the first time in a long while I could hear music and I knew it wasn't in my head — there were human voices singing Christmas carols and it wasn't a recording either. I stood up from the couch and saw a small choir gathered in the staff courtyard below. Their voices drifted up into the night and it was beautiful. I opened the window to hear better and smiled across at the nurses so they would know I wasn't going to jump out.

III. *Allegro scherzando*

After clearing up the breakfasts, I start the serious jobs I need to get done during my shift. I say 'serious' because washing up dishes in the little kitchen on B4 is light work compared to most of my other duties. Sometimes one of the patients will come and talk to me when I'm doing the dishes, perhaps even dry a few with me, although that's not really allowed. Some days, the hospital's catering manager — a nice Indian lady — will stop by to check the fridges. She's friendly, even to us cleaners, and likes to ask if the patients have enough healthy snacks. We'll have a quick yarn, if there's time before she rushes off again. I'm a great talker these days and I like to talk about music.

"Did you know Mozart had a sister who was also a child prodigy?" I asked Sally the psych nurse one day in the kitchen.

"Never heard of her," Sally muttered as she rifled through some patient's notes which had been left on the benchtop.

"She was taken on the early European tours along with Wolfgang. Their mother used to travel with them too. But you never hear what happened to her, or the mum."

Sally sniffed loudly, lifting her head to look at me. "You seem to know a lot about music — you play anything?"

"Not really," I said. "I'm more a Salieri than a Mozart," but I don't think she got what I meant.

For the serious cleaning, I have to get down on my hands and knees. I have long-handled mops and other equipment, but I prefer a couple of cloths and a bucket of warm soapy water. When I'm down on my knees I can see the grime up close. I can see this hospital is a mess. Raelene tells me it was never exactly flash — and the cheap tiles they used everywhere when they built this place have not worn well. Anything white soon looks old and grubby, but at least from my point of view I can see the dirt I'm trying to get rid of. Another reason I stopped using the long-handled mop was that there was this patient who used to follow me around shouting "Mop! Mop!" as I tried to clean the floor. He was one of the really mad ones and the other cleaners used to hide from him, but I tried singing to him instead. I've found that some music — it has to be the right song — will calm a psychotic patient. I tried suggesting to the nurses they should get a CD player or sound system for the ward, but they weren't interested in any advice from a cleaner.

I mainly work on the psych wards, but I have to be prepared to clean anywhere. Sometimes I have to go to Labour

Ward to help out and the cleaning there is hard work —
there's a lot of blood. Both my kids were born there, so I
know all about that. I don't mind the mess, the blood, shit
and vomit in my job, it's all just part of it. When I lost it after
Mum died, I gave up hope of a career in anything more
glamorous. I would have liked to have been a professional
pianist, or perhaps a music teacher, but the confidence to
perform, or to teach others, just disappeared. I left school
after my 'breakdown' (as Dad preferred to call it) and for
quite a while it was all I could do to get through each day.
Once I was on lower doses of meds I could function better,
think a bit more clearly, and after a few weeks I got work
as a cleaner at the local newspaper offices. As I cleaned
through the night and the papers rolled off the presses, the
grim headlines reminded me that my life wasn't so bad. It
was in that job that I started wearing headphones to listen
to music — that was the real start of my recovery.

Afternoons at the hospital are busy too. There's lots to get
done before I head off for the kids at 3 o'clock. Grant never
finishes work before 6 p.m., so he can't pick them up, but
I'm happy to leave work after six hours — it's part-time, but
it's long enough for me. On most wards, visiting is allowed
after 2 p.m., so I try to get my floor scrubbing done before
that. It's more difficult to clean with people in the way and
I'm also self-conscious about my singing. I don't like to
vocalise when I know others can hear, unless it's someone
who is so mad they don't know who I am or what I'm doing,
like Mop Man.

That reminds me, I saw Carl the other day as I was
rushing out of the hospital at the end of my shift. I don't

think he remembered me, but we had a quick chat about music.

"Did you know that Handel wrote an opera when he was only 18?" I asked Carl.

"Yes, *Almira* was his first," he replied. "But I think he was 19."

"What's it about?"

"It's about a medieval goddess." Carl started to sing some of it to me and Raelene in the hospital foyer. It sounded wonderful. I couldn't remember Carl singing on B4, but he had a great voice. Some of the visitors looked a bit alarmed, but it made me happy. There aren't many chances to hear live music when you've got littlies at home — I haven't been to a concert for years and I still don't go to church, although I love religious music. I'm a big fan of motets, which are like medieval madrigals. They were composed by women — one was Lucrezia Borgia's daughter — and were sung by nuns in sixteenth-century English convents. It is so moving, the sound of female voices in unison, and I find it comforting to know that women were singing together hundreds of years ago, before hospitals and cleaning equipment and modern life were invented.

One afternoon a week there's an assembly at Katie's school and parents are invited. It's a mad rush to get there, but once I'm in the school hall and listening to the children sing, I find I'm lost again. Not lost in a bad way, like I was after Mum died, but lost in the kingdom which music takes me to. It's a place where I can think more clearly and be myself. I can now see that my illness threw my brain out of control for a while, but that wasn't the real me. I now know that I am not my mother, and her destiny is not mine. I'm my children's mother and they are singing to me here in this draughty school hall. Katie is pelting out the notes with her little friends at the front of the hall and it melts my heart. Jacob is sitting on my knee singing "La la la la!" completely out of tune, but he's loving it.

When we get to the chorus, I sing too. Not too loud of course — I wouldn't want to attract any undue attention — but I sing with them. And I sing for them, and also for me.

~

The House Officer's Tale

~ LIZZIE ~

It seems to have been raining since the day I qualified, since the day in early autumn when I stepped onto this ward as Dr Sharpe. It came as quite a surprise to be called 'doctor' for the first time — I was walking over from the residences on my very first day when my pager went off for the first time. I answered hesitantly and the efficient voice on the other end asked if they were speaking to Dr Sharpe. Answering yes felt more like a question than an answer. I was told there was a patient on my ward (*my* ward!) who needed blood taking and an IV line replacing. Reality hit me: the buck stopped here now.

My hands shook as I gathered the equipment to perform my first procedure as an actual doctor. They shook some more as I placed the tourniquet around the patient's arm. I kept telling myself I had done this many times before as a student, but I felt sick with fear. I was frightened of harming my patient (*my* patient!) but also fearful of having to admit I couldn't do something doctors are supposed to be able to do. After I'd introduced myself, Mr Black made a comment about how young doctors seemed these days. I didn't tell him I'd just had my twenty-third birthday. As I wobbled the needle into his vein, I made small talk, pretending it wasn't my first day, pretending I knew what I was doing. As his blood flashed back into the narrow plastic tube, my whole body flushed with relief and I wanted to shout "Yes!" but I kept chatting about the weather. Another realisation: doctoring is an act. We spend years learning the science, but it's an art we are performing.

Later that day the fear subsided for a while when I met my colleagues — Matt the SHO and Michael the Med Reg — who have become my brothers-in-arms these last three months. Matt's from Invercargill and Michael's from Hong Kong and they have more in common than differences between them. They are both young and smart — this is the professorial medical team after all, and these jobs are hard to get, although we have yet to meet our esteemed leader as he's always away at conferences overseas, teaching other doctors how to be brilliant. Unlike me, Matt and Michael know what they are doing and they were quietly confident when they gave me my list of tasks on my first day. Essentially, I would do what they told me to do, report back to them and then get on with the next list. I should ask if I needed to, but it was implied that I shouldn't have to. It was clear from the start that I should do as instructed and not make any decisions about treatment or other interventions on my own. I was glad about that. The Med Reg is the decision-maker on our team, as the Prof is never here. There is another consultant on our team — a silver-haired man who appears from time to time to lead ward rounds — but he never speaks to me.

My house officer job consists of looking after the patients on a general medical ward: about thirty mainly elderly people, some with heart conditions, but they are mostly just old and ill and their bodies are failing them. Every day I review their notes, write up their drug charts, fix the pieces of plastic going into and out of their bodies (drips, catheters, other tubes), refer them for tests, ask more senior doctors to review them, and chase results. I am always chasing: chasing the forms I fill in, chasing results, chasing people to help with the results. Then I report back to Matt, and after that, I do all of these tasks again.

During an on-call day, I do my usual work but also admit new patients who are acutely unwell and have to come into hospital as a matter of urgency. Each one takes a lot of time, especially if they are confused, or semi-conscious, or have multiple problems — and often they are all three. I have to take their medical history, examine them, take their blood, order other investigations, set up IV lines, review and prescribe drugs and explain things to them and any caregivers attending.

Sometimes it's more dramatic than this and we have to resuscitate them before anything else can be done. During on-call days and night shifts, Matt, Michael and I carry the cardiac arrest pager which directs us to any collapsed patient in the hospital. There are usually two or three arrest calls during a typical shift. During the day, a crowd of people will attend, the most helpful of whom are the anaesthetists, as they are experts at intubation and I'm not great at sticking tubes into airways yet. Everything I know about resus I learned from the gas men. Dr Malik (whom I may now call

Anil) started our first tutorial by telling us to remember that anything we did at the scene of a cardiac arrest was positive — the patient is dead already. Initially that shocked me, but I've found this thought (always in Anil's quiet voice) calms me when I arrive at an arrest, especially if I'm the first to get there, especially in the middle of the night. The procedure is relatively straightforward: we run like hell to where we are directed and then begin the routine that has been drilled into us. Airway, Breathing, Circulation. It's not just ABC though: I'm learning it's really not like the diagrams in textbooks or practising on the resus dolls in carefully set-up seminar rooms.

Matt and I do a ward round each day and Michael joins us when he is not in clinic. Sometimes there is a round with one of the bosses and this is a more formal and tense affair, with a gaggle of people around each bed and led by The Master. We all have stories of our worst ward-round moments. My friend Mary felt faint during one extra-long round and tried to lean on the student next to her. He thought she was trying to come on to him and pushed her away, so she fainted right on top of the Professor — a slight man who fell over under the weight of a well-built woman. My story is similarly embarrassing — I was asked to look up a drug dose in front of the whole group and reached deep into my over-stuffed pocket for my phone. As I pulled it out, two tampons (thankfully unused) flipped onto the patient's bed and lay there on his lap. It was like an old *Carry On Doctor* movie, but not as funny. The consultant went white as I hastily reclaimed them and I wondered if perhaps he had never seen a tampon before.

We might laugh about such episodes later, but at the time ward rounds are the hours of judgment for junior doctors. Have we done all the necessary tests, have we got the results back, have we chased all the relevant people? Sometimes, but not always, we discuss if we have got the diagnosis right. The Master grills his apprentices, patronises the nurses, bullies his juniors and we all stand there and take it because for most of us, our next job depends on it. Sometimes my mind wanders and I look out at the rain and dare to dream that I might be doing something else, somewhere else, with someone else.

Loving

This summer, I was with someone else. While I was revising for my finals a few months ago, I met a guy in the med school library. Josh was a student in the year below mine and he was studying for exams too. I used to work upstairs in an area overlooking the trees beside the river — I called it the library sweet-spot as it had a view, not too much sun and was quieter than some of the communal areas which were too loud for me. He would occasionally ask me a question about something he was studying, but we didn't talk for long. I was surprised one day when he dropped a note on my table which read 'Coffee?' Nothing else, no name, no number. I looked up and he had disappeared, so I squiggled 'Yes' in red pen on his note, folded it and left it on the corner of my desk. It was hard to get back to work with those first grains of excitement stirring inside me, but I tried to play it cool. I carried on revising the cranial nerves, but I couldn't focus, I kept scanning the room for him. When he didn't reappear, it occurred to me he might have gone to the café on the ground floor, so I packed up my stuff and went tentatively downstairs with his note in my hand.

He was sitting near the windows, a cup of coffee and the students' magazine on the table in front of him. His head was down and his hair — long blond tresses, not too tidy — were catching the summer sunshine. He looked a bit like Jesus — or maybe an Australian surfer. I smiled at the thought of a surfing Jesus as I walked over to him, pleased I was wearing the new strappy sandals I'd found in an op shop, and gave him back his note. He looked up, opened the folded slip of paper, read my answer and smiled back at me. His eyes were bluer than they were upstairs. He really was gorgeous.

"Flat white, please," I said, trying not to look too keen.

"Sure." As he walked to the counter, he looked back over his shoulder. "I'm Josh, by the way."

"Lizzie," I called after him, but I wasn't sure he had heard.

When he came back with my coffee we sat facing each other and conversation came easily. We talked furiously about medicine, exams and studying. I talked more than he did, pulling at my hair (shorter than his and less golden), trying to look intelligent, but not too much so. Josh twisted his fingers around each other when he paused for thought. He had lovely hands. We both agreed we'd had enough of studying through this unusually sultry summer, when everyone else was outside enjoying themselves. As we talked, I began thinking this could be my last summer, as by autumn I would be qualified and that would be the end of youth, the end of fun. Not that I'd had much fun in my years at med school — it had been mainly work. I imagined Josh had had a better time: I pictured him surfing in summer, playing in a band, or hanging out with friends on a Friday night, not home alone reading up on neuro anatomy like me.

When we had finished our coffee, he suggested we take the rest of the day off and go for a drive in his car. It was only 11 a.m. and this wasn't something I would have normally considered, being an A student going for honours (I didn't just want to qualify, I wanted to be Top Doc) and also someone who didn't normally get into cars with guys I'd only just met. But I did sort of know him — from the library anyway — and I felt like doing something different. It was more than that: I wanted to rebel, do something bad. I wasn't feeling myself that day, it was as if I was becoming someone else — and it felt good.

We drove through the outskirts of town, away from the uni, the hospital and our lives there. Josh's old wreck rattled as he clunked through the gears. I was happy not to be in the driving seat, which again was odd for me, and I felt a surge of freedom and optimism. My normal self would have been expecting him to abduct and murder me, leaving my body in a ditch by the road. We talked about all sorts of things, including art and religion — he was a Christian, but didn't try to convert me — and about books which were not about medicine. We discovered we both loved literature, as in fiction. He liked Graham Greene and Lloyd Jones, I loved Hilary Mantel and Keri Hulme. We discussed the perspectives of male and female novelists and I realised it had been a long time since I'd thought about anything other than the malfunctioning of the human body. We drove on, the hospital where I would soon be working still just in view, but we didn't talk about what it might be like to be a doctor.

It was a bright blue-green day, the sea glistening in the distance. The weight of studying, hunched over my laptop in the stuffy library, was evaporating, blown away in the breeze from the open car windows. When Josh started talking about some of his favourite surfing beaches, his head tilting towards me, golden locks oscillating, I felt a sudden urge to touch him and reached across to stroke his leg. I placed my hand just above his knee, half expecting him to jump back, pull away. He didn't jump. Maybe I had him trapped. Josh was a relaxed driver, only one hand on the wheel at any time, and we continued to chat about fiction and surfing (and surfing fiction) as I started to explore a small tear in his cotton shorts. He reached over to me, his left hand now on my right thigh. I stroked the back of his hand and we drove on like this, both smiling absurdly and not talking so much now.

We stopped at a place I had been a few times before — a park, more like a field with long billowing grass in summer, which has views over the city below and out to sea. It's one of those places you might go to think about life, or to grieve for a loved one, but it wasn't sad that first day I went there with Josh. We lay in the grass and stroked each other, then we kissed with increasing intensity, until the insides of me felt utterly disturbed. As his tongue pushed into my mouth, my heart jittered — what arrhythmia was this, for God's sake? — and my breathing became loud in my ears.

He was clumsy, his hands on my breasts, on my butt, his fingers lifting up my flimsy skirt. I could feel his erection against my stomach and found myself begging him to fuck me. Those words were not mine, yet now they were. He fumbled around a bit more, unzipped his shorts and penetrated me urgently. It was fast and furious and he came too soon, saying "Sorry," as he rolled away from me into the long grass. I lay there looking up at the blue sky, wondering what had just happened.

* * *

The rest of summer passed in a similar way, except that it was a bit more controlled and co-ordinated. After that first episode of unprotected sex (so unprotected! so unexpected!) in the great outdoors, I went to the family planning clinic to get myself sorted. Josh was organising one of his Medical Student Christian Group activities that evening. The doctor who saw me, Prof White, had been one of my gynae tutors and I asked her why it was called a family planning clinic when none of us attending were planning families, quite the opposite. She laughed and I giggled and I didn't mention that I had failed to use any contraception that first time with Josh (I thought she might lower my grade). I nodded seriously when she explained all the contraceptive options and talked about STDs which I thought only other people would get. Feeling fully protected and generally invincible, I left the clinic humming a happy tune and planning a summer of sex.

In the mornings Josh and I would study at the library for a few hours and then we would walk back to his flat, in an old villa near the river. His flatmates were often out, so we had the place to ourselves, meaning we could have loud, invigorating and exhausting sex. God, it was fun. We laughed a lot and usually ended up on his bed in a room filled with late-afternoon sun, lying in the smells of our bodies and sipping water out of an old wine bottle that still smelled vaguely of alcohol. It was on this bed I first saw his body properly, as we lay together on one of those first afternoons. He really did have the most beautiful torso — it was like one of the those sculptures you see in museums, the muscles well defined by the hours he spent surfing before he met me. I told him his body was perfect for our anatomy revision, but it wasn't really, because it was several decades younger than most of the patients we practised on. My body was young, but I didn't like it much — my thighs were too fat and my breasts too small — so I used the sheets to hide these parts from Josh. All summer, in that house by the river, I drew lines along his muscles with my fingers and kissed his chest, stroked his thighs. I studied his penis: I became fascinated by it, how it responded to me. I worshipped his body and couldn't pull myself away. In our quieter moments I wanted to tell him I loved him, yet it always seemed too soon.

Sometimes we went out for a couple of drinks at one of the student watering holes, delighting in being with each other in public, his hand on the small of my back, my hand stroking his hair, or draping myself over him when I became giggly from the booze. On Tuesday evenings and Sunday mornings Josh did things with his Christian friends, while I dashed back to my flat to do laundry. But mainly we stayed together, in his bedroom through those long summer afternoons and evenings. When his flatmates came home we could hear them joking that Josh had taken someone hostage, but I didn't want to see anyone else, so we stayed in his room, sometimes talking and reading to each other, often just lying together. Our nights were intimate too: sometimes I would wake at 3 a.m. and watch him, thinking about how much I loved him, until I fell asleep again. In the morning when it was time to go to the library to study, or for me to go to the hospital for clinical cases, we showered together before we left the house, lingering as long as we could before returning to our real worlds.

I'm not sure how I passed my finals, but I did. I survived all the written papers and verbal interrogations and almost got Honours. Josh took his exams too and then told me he was leaving for Vanuatu. Or that's how it seemed at the time. Now I can see that he had mentioned his ten-week student elective earlier in our relationship, but on that day — the day of his last exam, when I had thought we would be celebrating — it felt like a nuclear bomb had landed on my world. Deeply in love, plagued by midsummer madness, I did not play it cool. I begged him not to go, I cried and clung onto him as he explained it was his destiny. His destiny! Was I not his destiny? Josh was a reverend's son and his life ambition was to work for a Christian NGO in a country much poorer than ours. His Pacific Island elective would be the start of his dream career. We had talked about destinies as we lay on his bed during the long summer afternoons. We had discussed the role of religion in his life after reading *The End of the Affair* together, his hand stroking my hair as my head lay on his chest, our bodies entwined and inseparable (or so I thought). I had not seriously believed he would leave me to go to Vanuatu, even if it was only for ten weeks. Ten weeks! It might as well have been forever. I had thought he would stay with me. I thought that he loved me and that love conquered all, even a man's destiny to save the world. I was wrong.

Longing

After Josh left, I wondered whether I'd been wrong to think that he loved me, how I had got it so wrong, but most of all I longed for him. I longed for him with my whole body: I missed him with my entire being. I felt weak, my chest was caving in, my legs were not strong enough to raise me from the bed where I lay in my flat, looking out at the rain. I didn't go to the airport with him, I stayed in bed wearing his jumper and I cried for three days. My flat-mate Sharmila was kind. She sat on my bed and listened while I asked her if he had really loved me; whether if he had really loved me, would he have left me? She passed me tissues as I sobbed that I loved Josh and just wanted to marry him and have his children. As a feminist, Sharmila couldn't resist saying that marriage was a patriarchal institution and I would do well to have none of it. I didn't listen. Instead, I questioned myself — if I really loved Josh, wouldn't I have gone to Vanuatu with him? He hadn't asked me to go, but shouldn't I just book a flight and go out there and turn up in his clinic, as would happen in a trashy novel? Sharmila pointed out I had just qualified as a doctor and was due to start my first job next week. This was just about enough to lift the fog of my longing and the next day I got out of bed for a few hours. I went up to the park above the town where we had made love that first day. I looked out to sea and cried some more.

During that time after Josh flew away from me, I thought I was pregnant. My period, always so regular, did not arrive on time. Sharmila pointed out I had lost a lot of weight during my summer of love — she had studied nutrition and knew that not eating enough can stop our reproductive cycles. I picked at the curries she made me try, but couldn't taste anything anymore. I phoned the family planning clinic (I couldn't face seeing Prof White again) and a pleasant-sounding nurse asked if I felt pregnant. I didn't know. How did it feel to be pregnant? I certainly felt sick and tired and I'd found it hard to get up in the mornings since Josh left. I knew I should just go out and buy a test, but part of me didn't want to know. There was some comfort in thinking there might be a part of him left inside me.

I wrote to Josh repeatedly, telling him how much I still loved him. My emails were longer than most of the essays I had written in my finals and in my mind they relived so much of the beautiful time we had spent together. I still wore his jumper. The rain still came down. I felt close to him as I tapped away at my laptop. He did not reply. Sharmila said that perhaps he hadn't received my messages, perhaps the internet was unreliable in Vanuatu, but I knew these were not the reasons for his silence. As grey droplets ran down the windows and we sipped endless cups of tea, Sharmila and I discussed male and female perspectives on love. We concluded that men seem to be able to carry on with their lives in the face of love and longing. They don't seem to feel the desperation we feel.

My period arrived on the day I left my flat to move into the hospital residences, so although it was uncomfortable lifting boxes, it was also good timing, I guess. My dad drove over to help me move and I cried when he arrived. I was glad he didn't tell me I looked terrible, which my mother would have done. He just started putting my boxes and bags into his car and when this was done, he suggested we get a burger on the way to the hospital. We sat eating and watching the rain, me wearing Josh's jumper — which I still hadn't washed — and feeling utterly miserable. My dad talked about his work (he isn't a doctor) and a bit about Mum and my brothers and what was going on at home. Everyone's lives were carrying on as normal, while I was trying to scramble out of the bomb crater that was now mine. I didn't tell Dad about Josh or anything else and he was still chatting, still carrying on as normal, when he left me in my new room in the residences the night before I started my new job.

Working

The anxiety surrounding my first days as a house officer temporarily displaced my grief over Josh. Didn't someone wise say that work is the cure for personal misery, or something like that? I only wore Josh's jumper in the evenings, when I wasn't on call and was back in my room alone, collapsed on the bed. I was so tired I fell asleep within half an hour of getting back to my room, so I wasn't awake to miss him. But I missed him in my sleep and longed for him when I woke.

The first months of my first job ground on. I was tired all the time; I am still tired all the time. I've become reasonably efficient at clerking new patients, doing my rounds, ticking off all my tasks — I now know a junior doctor's work is mostly filling in forms — and I need to ask Matt and Michael fewer questions these days. M and M (as I like to call them) are still my brothers-in-arms, still my heroes in this war zone of general internal medicine. Our first week of nights can only be described as a battle we fought together, with me, the useless new recruit, running around doing what I was told, but not doing it very well. I roamed the corridors, looking for blood gas machines, on-call technicians, food to eat, and learning that a hospital does not stay fully open all hours. I learned how to survive at 3 a.m., disoriented with fatigue and with hours of work ahead.

By the time of the fourteenth cardiac arrest that week, we were all exhausted. It was Sunday night, early Monday morning, and the nightmares just would not end. Our patient was lying collapsed on the ward floor near the toilet, and Matt and Michael were performing ABC and all the other letters of resuscitation, assisted by the on-call anaesthetist. It wasn't Anil Malik that night, but I could hear him talking us quietly through what was happening. I watched as the patient was intubated, his lungs insufflated with oxygen. Matt straddled the patient giving cardiac compressions until sweat dripped off his forehead and Michael asked us to stand clear for defibrillation. But it was all for nothing — our patient's heart had given up. I knelt on the floor holding Mr Black's hand. I couldn't think of anything else to do.

Now I feel old. I've been a doctor for three months, but it feels like years since I was a med student passing notes in the library, abandoning my studies for fun in a field not too far from here. I've come to know the anatomy and physiology of this dilapidated hospital and understand the part I play in its life. Its structures are failing — last week I noticed more stains had appeared on the walls of my ward, near the toilets. Yet somehow we keep it going. And *we* keep going, our small band of twenty-somethings who work these ungodly hours, the nights the managers sleep comfortably in their beds at home. I try not to think about God because I don't want to think about all the deaths I've witnessed these last few months. Death is my life now. I also don't want to think about Josh, serving his God far away from me, although he may be back by now. I haven't missed him so much recently.

The number of hours I'm at work doesn't allow me to think much anyway. There is no time to consider different perspectives. I just follow routines and protocols and my main objective is surviving being a junior doctor. Every week I spend hours with Matt, more time than I spend with anyone else, and we sometimes get the chance to talk. It's mainly hospital stuff, but one night in the mess we were having a chat about all sorts of things, including what we missed.

"I miss being a normal person," Matt said, and I raised my eyebrows knowingly towards Michael and Anil, who were with us on the corner couches. We were eating cold pizza we'd had delivered earlier that evening. It was 3 a.m. again.

"You were never normal, mate," said Michael, who makes an effort to sound more Kiwi than he really is.

"I miss taking a shit without being interrupted," Matt continued and started to expand on his theories about how bowel action is affected by being on call and sleep deprivation.

"T.M.I!" I was trying to eat my pizza and didn't want to consider Matt's hypothesis any further. He was absolutely right anyway. "I miss eating proper food at normal times," I continued, then stopped, realising I was sounding like Sharmila, or maybe my mum.

Anil was unusually quiet that night. In fact, he was acting a bit weird. He was on his phone a lot, which wasn't like him, so I tried to say something interesting to get his attention.

"I think we've all been institutionalised at too young an age, don't you?"

"I'm too old to still be working nights," Anil muttered and carried on texting.

"I miss my wife," Mike said. There was a slightly awkward silence, so he added quickly "and Hong Kong food. So delicious!"

Matt poked his finger into one of the holes in the couch. "I miss Anna. I think she might be going to dump me."

I almost told them about Josh, but we were interrupted by another crash call.

* * *

Now I can lead the cardiac arrest team if I have to, if M and M are not around, if others are busy. I tell myself — and any students following me around on the ward — that everything we do is positive, we can only try our best. I know my As, Bs and Cs, and can now do them in a real life (or death) situation. Most of the time I can intubate, and if I can't, I don't panic: I slide the tube back out of the patient's throat, position their head correctly and return to bag and mask, as Anil taught me. It usually works, but I've also learned there is often nothing we can do. I still like to hold my patients' hands when I can, but mostly there's no time for long encounters. I'd still rather be holding Josh's hand, but the longing has eased and I am recovering. The jumper he left with me has finally been washed and put away.

~

The Theatre Sister's Tale

~ DENISE ~

It was far too beautiful a day to be diagnosed with cancer. As the early morning mist lifted from the harbour, the water began to sparkle and a crisp, clear day lay ahead. She had felt optimistic as she fed Gregory, who had been out and about early, chasing birdsong around the garden. Rusty leaves fluttered to the ground from the birch near her window, its silver-white trunk stark in the sunlight. Denise noticed a few wax-eyes flitting about in the almost-naked branches and thought then that she hadn't heard the shining cuckoo this week. Winter was on its way. As Gregory settled into cleaning his paws and tail — an artform he was ever perfecting — Denise finished her cup of tea, locked up the house and drove into town towards the hospital.

The clinic was busy, but the staff were cheerful.

"Lovely day out there," someone said as Denise joined the queue at the desk.

"There was a frost at our place this morning," one of the receptionists commented, "but I guess we've got to expect that now."

Denise didn't join in the chit-chat. She didn't know any of the staff in this outpatient clinic, as she had spent the last twenty years working deep within the inpatient departments. Her world, her life, had been the operating theatres on Level 5, where as a senior sister she had become something of an institution. Not a popular institution, she knew, and this had been commented upon in the meeting earlier that week when all the theatre staff — except the surgeons, of course — had been told they would have to reapply for their own jobs. It had been a bombshell to everyone, especially the older staff like Denise, who had known a time when the hospital management hadn't questioned the need to treat them with some respect.

Denise did not want any more bombshells this week, or next for that matter. She would reapply for her own job, if that's what she had to do. The union was telling its members they shouldn't have to sing to the managers' tune and all the rest, but Denise wasn't in the union. In her view they created more problems than they solved for the hospital's workforce. She had told the younger nurses not to join: they shouldn't rely on a bunch of socialists to save their jobs — they needed to look after themselves. This was one of the opinions which made her unpopular with the other theatre staff, who seemed to get along much better with each other than they did with her. She knew some of them whispered behind her back in the changing rooms at the beginning of shifts, when they stuffed their over-treated hair into the dishcloth-blue theatre hats, gawping at themselves in the mirror and applying mascara and lipstick as finishing touches. Make-up in an operating theatre! What were they coming to work for? To find a husband? Or maybe these days it was a lesbian lover.

They called her 'old-school' because she wouldn't wear the disposable hats they all wore and preferred a traditional white cotton wrap, which she had always used. She didn't suggest the young ones protect their hair in this way. They wouldn't listen to old-fashioned ideas anyway: they wanted progress and they probably thought they had it with their throw-away hats and electronic Christmas cards and people from all corners of the globe working at the hospital. Half the staff were Asian these days. Denise could tolerate the Indian anaesthetist — at least he was polite and punctual — but they really were employing anyone now. There was a new theatre porter who could hardly speak English, and the clinical directors had recently appointed a female prof of O&G. Women didn't make good surgeons, in Denise's opinion: juggling all the demands of a highly technical career with long hours and family commitments was just too much for them. It wasn't a politically correct view, she knew, but she thought mothers should be at home with their children. She doubted Sarah White would last the course and wondered what had happened to all the nice Kiwi boys they used to encourage into medical school.

* * *

Finally, Denise reached the front of the queue at the clinic's reception.

"Mrs Rogers for a 9.30 appointment with Mr Parkins," she reported to the clerk, a vacuous-looking girl whose name badge told everyone she was called Courtney.

"Thank you, Mrs Rogers, please take a seat." Courtney did not take her eyes off the screen in front of her. Denise took a chair in the corner of the waiting area. Looking around, she thought how shabby this outpatient clinic was compared to her shiny theatres. It was dirty too: she studied the marks on the floor and the smears on the windows. She wouldn't let her cleaners off so lightly. She was glad her colleagues upstairs didn't know about the colonoscopy she'd finally had a week ago, because of her rectal bleeding. It wasn't something she wanted to discuss with anyone, and she was now hoping that today would be the last time it would dominate her thoughts. Every day, every night, for weeks it had been there, and she wanted it to go away. The presence of symptoms had been a new experience for Denise. She'd had a lifetime of good health — apart from the usual coughs and colds — and used to brag to the junior theatre staff that she hadn't had a day off sick in forty years. The younger ones were always off with something or other and if it wasn't them who were sick, it was their sniffly, snotty kids.

It was not until Denise noticed the shocking blood, incarnadine in the toilet pan, that the earlier vague sensations of worry solidified into the realisation that her body was malfunctioning. The worry ground on during the week she waited for an appointment with her GP, and it writhed around inside her when he asked about changes in bowel habit. Yes, now she thought about it, there had been changes and yes, she had lost weight. Then she worried more through the weeks of waiting for the colonoscopy and a CT scan. She had been offered the chance to go private, but baulked at having to pay for healthcare she had been providing all her working life to others who got it for free.

Denise saw the news was bad before she heard it. Mr Parkins sat stiffly at his desk and would not meet her eyes as she walked into his consulting room. There wasn't much else for him to look at in the box-like space, just a few cracked tiles around the wash basin in the corner, but he managed to avoid eye contact quite well, fingering the corners of the clinical notes in front of him. When he did eventually look at her, she wondered if he recognised her from theatre. She knew JEP fairly well — although he wasn't one of her surgeons — but often the consultants looked right through the nurses (even the sisters, their most valued handmaidens) or looked at them in ways that Denise did not welcome. It had been many years since anyone had tried it on with her, but she noticed how the older men still looked at the younger nurses, how they leered if they thought they could. Some things never changed.

"It's a rectal carcinoma. And the staging looks like Dukes C," he said bluntly. His loud voice was used to being listened to.

Denise could not speak. Another bombshell after all. Mr Parkins continued to lecture her and although his lips were moving, she couldn't hear what he was saying. How suddenly she had become a patient and how unsettling it felt. She wanted to ask why doctors use words like carcinoma or neoplasm or tumour or malignancy, when they should just tell you that you have cancer. He must know I'm a nurse to put it like that, Denise thought, but I still don't understand. Was this her body he was talking about in such technical terms?

She knew Dukes C meant that the cancer had spread through the bowel wall, that she would need radical surgery and chemotherapy: weeks and months of treatment that would emaciate her, sicken her, give her endless diarrhoea, make her anaemic and vulnerable to infection, and she would probably lose her hair too. And after all that she might die anyway. She had seen it happen to others. Mr Parkins didn't tell her any of the possible complications, only that he would do the surgery.

"I'll chop it out!" he said abruptly, with an unnerving excess of enthusiasm. She thought he might be about to use a rugby analogy to explain his proposed interventions further, but after pausing for breath — he was by now quite red in the face — he just declared, "We'll fix you up!"

Denise wondered why he was bellowing around the tiny room: his only audience was herself and a young nurse who was waiting around uncertainly, seemingly unsure as to what to do. And then he seemed in a hurry — he got up out of his chair and made towards the door, telling Denise that the oncologist would speak to her later. She wasn't asked what she wanted or how she felt — but she didn't know how she felt anyway. Sitting in that alien white environment on a plastic clinic chair, on the wrong side of the doctor's desk, she felt detached, as if this was someone else's cancer they were talking about.

After she was dismissed, Denise left the hospital by the main entrance. She didn't usually exit this way — there were other ways out, nearer to the theatre suites, and the reception area was always busy with too many people coming and going. Today was no exception and there was even some loony singing to that receptionist who smiles too much. This place was getting worse by the day. Denise hurried out, found her car and drove towards home. Random thoughts kept crashing in as she went through the motions of driving. Two bombshells, two threats of the chop in one week. Her life — hitherto so straightforward and predictable — was in pieces now — and it had all happened in just a few days. But she knew that wasn't true. Everything revealed to her this week had been a long time coming. The decision to make so many of them redundant must have required a *Progressing Change* exercise. And the biological changes within her, her own cellular multiplications and modifications, which had now metamorphosed into cancer, would have taken time too. She hadn't been aware, but now she knew.

Denise pulled over in a parking bay beside the harbour. She needed to get her thoughts in order. It was quiet after the engine was turned off, just some seabirds squawking. She watched them soaring and swooping and diving for fish; she could smell the krill, floating pink in the shallows and dried out on the rocks. Denise was not used to sitting around in the middle of the day — this was only her second day off sick in years and she never took all her annual leave. Even when Bill had been so ill, all that time ago, she had still gone into work, every single day she was rostered.

Now she had the rest of the day to herself, but it was wasted. Who needs a day off to be told they have cancer? Disgusting, invasive, terminal cancer. Mr Parkins had said he would fix her up, but she knew he couldn't, and even if he could, she knew the cost. As she looked over the bay, she realised that soon there would be lots more days off work, away from the routines that were her life. There were all the treatments to come — the surgery, the chemo — although maybe they wouldn't treat her, as in cure her, maybe they would just make her sicker. That's what happened to Bill, after all. Would she ever recover? If she recovered this time, what then? She had seen enough operations over enough years to know that cancer comes back. Denise had watched Bill die.

Looking back towards town, across the water, she could just about see the hospital. It was easy to pick out when there was a helicopter landing on its roof: a noisy metallic insect carrying another life to be saved within those walls. Or maybe not. She started thinking about all the bodies, all the souls, who had passed through that exhausted building in this city at the bottom of the world. Some lives saved, other lives ending. All ending in the end.

A train rumbled in the distance and she thought about the metal trolleys in which the deceased were removed from theatre, or from the wards, to be taken to the hospital mortuary. How their bodies were placed in those grey steel boxes so that other patients wouldn't see the dead. But she had seen the dead and she had seen them die. Dying in a hospital operating theatre was not a pretty way to go. Even after all the tubes and lines were removed and the walls of the corpse were pulled back together by the surgeons who had lost their battle with life this time, the bodies were ugly. They had been mutilated by the people trying to save them, by the drugs pumped into them, and by the diseases that had eaten them away.

Denise knew she did not want to die that way. It wasn't just the thought of a painful recovery from radical surgery and the horrible side effects of chemotherapeutic agents, all of which Bill had suffered. It was also the fact that her whole undignified demise would be witnessed by others. There would be weeks when she would attend the oncology unit and sit in those over-comfortable chairs donated by charities and well-wishers (as if a comfy chair and an expensive TV could ease the process of dying from cancer) and be looked after by kind and efficient nurses, as they hooked her up to drugs which would not be a miracle cure. Other kind and elderly volunteers would ask, "And how are you today?" and she would neither be able to smile and say, "I'm good, thanks," nor "Piss off and leave me alone while I die in peace."

Then there would be the days when she lay on theatre trolleys and in hospital beds, surrendering control of her fate to the staff who would take her blood, cut her skin, remove her organs. She would be put in machines and scanned and examined. The witnesses would tell her to be a good patient, not to worry, and would give her leaflets about support groups.

The witnesses would be unknown to her. There wouldn't be anyone crying at her bedside or holding her hand as her life came to an end. Bill wouldn't be there, as she had been for him. They hadn't had children — his cancer had left him sterile — and Denise had no other family. Her parents had smoked themselves to death and she had been an only child. Since Bill, all that time ago, she had lived her life alone, mostly out of choice. Friends and neighbours were fine if they kept their distance. She knew most of her colleagues didn't like her much, but that made it easier now. Her possible redundancy made things less painful too. No one needed her any more and no one else would have to suffer with her through whatever happened next.

Denise suddenly realised what she had to do. She was still sitting in her car beside the harbour, but if she left now, she could get there before they closed the road at 3 p.m. As she drove, she thought how ridiculous it was that the road to the heads was closed in the mid-afternoon. Those intending to die there could easily park their car and walk the last few hundred metres to the top to throw themselves off. Or if they were really determined, could they not just drive through the barrier at high speed and up and over and off the clifftop, like Thelma and Louise?

But life, like death, is different in the movies. When it comes to it, how many people can take their own lives? Denise thought she could. She briefly considered Gregory, but someone would take him in, or take him to the SPCA — or maybe he would just leave home and look after himself. She hadn't spoken to her neighbours in months, but the comings and goings of their cars told her they still lived next door. Eventually someone would realise she wasn't coming back. Denise thought about whether she should write a note, or more detailed letters to put her affairs in order. She had made a will years ago — she and Bill had gone to a solicitor together when they knew he hadn't got much longer. All her assets were to go to the SPCA, so that was sorted. Any other details would take time and she knew she had to do this now. Someone else could take care of the rest once she was gone.

It was still a beautiful day as she pulled up at the top of the road to the heads, above the cliffs. Fluffy white clouds were settling on the summits of distant hills. The sun was low and blinding, slowly descending towards the blurry line where sky and sea become one, where it would then disappear. The few remaining people on the beach far below were walking back towards their homes and lives in the settlement that nestled behind the furthest sand dunes. There would be no more cars, now that the barrier was down. There would be no witnesses. Denise parked her car, got out, and leaving the keys inside, shut the door firmly. She walked away from it towards the clifftop. A cold breeze caught her hair and the sea sparkled into infinity as she looked up. It was not too beautiful a day to die.

~

The Cook's Tale

This is a story about food. To be more specific, it's about my job as our hospital's catering services manager, which may sound like an uninspiring and not-so-glamorous part of the healthcare system, but please, let me try to persuade you otherwise. This is also my story. I am Sharmila Packiyanathan, a cook from Sri Lanka who has crossed the world and back again, fuelled by my love of food. Let me share some of my recipes for life with you.

I manage the team of people who feed the patients and staff, 24/7 (our kitchens never have a day off), but my job title doesn't really describe who I am. I am a cook. I learned from my grandmother, when I was very young and before our family had to leave our homeland. My grandmother would not have called herself a cook, although she spent hours every day preparing food in our home and I was always with her, watching and absorbing. My earliest memories are of her knees, knobbly and ageing. I would follow her around the kitchen until she finally had enough of me under her feet and would sweep me up to a seat at the table, where I was allowed to assist her with various tasks. At first I was not much help at all, but that didn't stop her giving me proper jobs like grinding spices and washing and trimming vegetables.

I can only have been two or three when I started helping my grandmother and I picked up all the basics from her. Years later, when I was training as a chef in kitchens far removed from my grandparents' Sri Lankan home, her quiet insistent voice — always reminding me of the correct way to wash or slice or grind — was ever with me. She would have been horrified at the carelessness of some of my peers, kitted out in fancy white jackets, but unable to detect the ripeness of fruit. She would be upset to see how children these days are kept out of the kitchen, far removed from their food, which is then presented to them to eat in front of the TV or computer screen. Sometimes I'm glad I don't have children, because I worry that I wouldn't be able to give them what my grandparents and parents gave me.

Growing up in Sri Lanka was a gift. At work, in our hospital, I am often taken for being Indian, but I always cheerfully explain that I was born on the teardrop-shaped island which drips off the end of India. I got this description from my father, who always spoke beautifully and often in the voice of one of his favourite Sri Lankan authors. My father used to say that Sri Lanka is at the centre of the world: just look at a map which has Britain upper left and New Zealand lower right — Sri Lanka is right in the middle. It certainly was the centre of our world until we had to leave, because our lives were at risk. We fled to Britain in 1977, during a particularly difficult period of the troubles. Things had been getting worse for a while: the explosions, the disappearances were getting closer to home. My mother no longer let us play in our street. It became too dangerous to stay. I was nine when we migrated and left my gift behind.

Our first years in the UK were not easy — we didn't fit in easily in the cold northern town where brown skins were uncommon and the kids at my school said we smelt funny. My father was a doctor and he got a position as a GP without too much trouble. Word soon spread that he was competent and kind and gentle, even if he was a Paki and smelt of curry. We lived a fairly middle-class British life — my sister and I went to a well-thought-of public (as in private) school, but we didn't board and came home each day to help my mother in the kitchen and eat meals together. English food was so different: so grey — like the weather — until we added my grandmother's blend of spices with terracotta-coloured turmeric to lift the dullness and fill our kitchen with the aromas of home.

Here's my Ammamma's quick-and-easy curry powder recipe for you: place one tablespoon of coriander seeds, two of cumin seeds, two of fennel seeds and one of fenugreek in a heavy-based pan and heat on a low flame for about five minutes, or until you smell the spices. You can add some dried chilli flakes, but you don't have to, as not all curries are hot. Then take it off the heat and stir in a good pinch of turmeric — maybe half a teaspoon for really intense colour — before you grind all the spices to a fine powder. You can use an electric grinder, but I prefer my pestle and mortar, it's more therapeutic. My grandmother's curry powder will flavour all sorts of meat and vegetable dishes, so use it liberally!

To get back to my story, when I finished school in England I still wanted to be a chef, although my teachers and parents were keen for me to become a doctor. Apparently, I was too clever to cook. Looking back now, I find this ridiculous, because being a chef requires a lot of intelligence, and the training in some ways is as hard as a medical one. However, I know they wanted the best for me and they were right to try to protect me from the prospects of long hours of hard work in poor conditions with low salaries. We reached a compromise — I went to university to study nutrition — which my parents hoped would lead me into a well-paid job in food science — but after three years I still wanted to be a chef.

I enjoyed university where I was no longer just a Paki girl and I met other Sri Lankan Tamils who missed their homeland too. Sometimes we cooked a feast of curries for our white friends — there was one girl who teasingly called me Sharmila the Tiger during the period when the civil war was featured on the British news. I liked her enough to spend time trying to correct the perceptions that were being reported from Sri Lanka in those days. For what seemed like years, but was only months in the end, Suzie and I lazed around on floor cushions drinking cheap wine and sharing all our secrets. She was passionate about everything and was the leader of the university's Amnesty International group, which I joined so I could spend more time with her. I loved her in ways I could not explain to anyone else.

At the end of my degree I was restless about my future, but I knew I didn't want a job in a lab inventing new ways to make fresh food last longer. I still wanted to cook, to be creative with food, to please people with my creations. So I was allowed to enrol at a hospitality school in the home counties, where the staff were too posh to admit their intake was mainly kids from middle-class families who didn't know what else to do with their lives. The 'intensive' cookery course lasted for six months, but it was lax compared to my grandmother's regime. The main thing I grasped was a boyfriend, and a young man called Rupert who came from a nearby town (which the locals liked to call a village) soon became my husband. We were married in great formality in a medieval church on the outskirts of his home town. The church was difficult to find, due to the number of roundabouts which had been constructed as the town was developed for twentieth-century life, but as Rupert's mother told me, it was worth the drive. Sitting on a small green hill, its spire reaching towards the heavens, a covered wooden gate admitting worshippers to the sanctuary of its graveyard, it was a storybook place. A safe place. The British take their churches for granted: they've always been there and no one is going to blow them up or tear them down.

The vicar didn't ask if I was a Christian (I wasn't) and to Rupert's family it mattered less than the guest list and the details of gifts we were asking our friends to buy from an expensive department store. Rupert's parents managed all the arrangements and I just went along with it, caught up in the excitement of being a bride, or perhaps just infected by the enthusiasm of others. My family travelled south for the wedding and stayed at a mid-range hotel where the bleached-blond proprietor sniffed loudly each time we passed through Reception. The reasons for our marrying in the south were said to be because Rupert and I had both just finished our training, but it was also because I felt my home was far away. Although the northern town of my schooldays didn't offer a picturesque church on a green hill, it was more of a home to me than mini-roundabout land, but my real home was even further away, in Colombo, where my Ammamma still cooked curries every day.

After the wedding and honeymoon — we went to a Caribbean island on a charter flight full of other British honeymooners — our parents helped us with the deposit for a tiny terraced house in Rupert's home town. I found myself work in busy hotel and restaurant kitchens in and around London. Being a brown woman in a white male environment meant I had to start at the bottom, washing and cleaning before progressing to prepare any food. However, with time, I was able to demonstrate my skills — my grandmother had taught me well — and there were those who recognised I could be useful and taught me more. I rose through the ranks to become a sous-chef and after a few more years I actually became the head chef at a boutique hotel which then became known for its 'Western adaptations of Eastern dishes'. It was still unusual for a woman to have such a job (I felt like a fraud in the first months when my staff called me Chef) and for this reason I was featured in one of the Sunday supplements. A journalist and photographer came to do a photo-shoot at the hotel and it was all very exciting. The food writer revealed she had eaten in our restaurant the previous week as a secret diner and had loved my curries. She asked me for a recipe to include in the article, so I shared my one for dahl, which is easy to make in a home kitchen and is also comforting in times of trouble. It has an extra ingredient which makes it different to other dahl recipes: I add crushed coriander seeds to the spice mix, which lifts it to a new level. Trust me, it's wonderful! You can also add fresh coriander leaves on top, just before serving.

That Sunday I became a small-time celebrity in the big-time London kitchen scene. People were talking about me at home too. My parents cut out the glossy photo of their daughter in her crisp white chef's outfit (it looked wonderful against my chocolate skin) and put it on their fridge. I wondered when the news would reach Sri Lanka, but I knew it wouldn't take long. My mother would be on the phone, boasting about her famous daughter before teatime.

The art of being a wife did not go so well. It became clear after our brief honeymoon period that we were not compatible. Rupert gave up cooking quite soon after we married and found more highly paid but flavourless em-ployment as a stockbroker in the city. He was influenced by his family and once they began to see that their Indian princess image of me (which suited them at first, although I kept explaining I was from Sri Lanka) was tainted, they soon found much to criticise. They didn't want me to work — especially not in a kitchen — they thought that Rupert should keep me and I should keep house — a nice tidy house, where it would be absolutely fine to be in the kitchen — and have babies, hopefully four, but at least two to start with. I didn't agree.

"I want to earn my own money," I said during a particularly terse conversation over dinner at his family mansion, where I sat at my specifically allocated daughter-in-law position at the dining room table. Actually, it hadn't been a conversation up until this point. They had been lecturing me, telling me how it was, how it should be, not expecting a response. But I had to respond, so I continued as the family finished their lemon syllabub — made by Mummy and quite frankly a bit average, it needed more zest.

"Isn't it better for women to be paid for working in a professional kitchen, rather than not being paid for slaving at home?"

There was a disapproving silence, followed by nervous laughter from the sisters. Daddy was looking uncomfortable and Rupert was shifting in his seat. If only he could have supported me. They had finished their dessert, but I was still struggling with mine. The other women at the table got up to clear the dishes and take them to the kitchen. I stayed where I was. As they left the dining room, I could hear Rupert's mother whispering to one of the sisters, "Is she one of those feminists?"

When they returned to the table, I spoke quietly and calmly, although I felt upset inside.

"Sri Lankan women are strong and central in our families, but hopefully we are not oppressed. In this way I see myself as a feminist." There was another awkward silence.

"Oh gosh, I hope you aren't going to burn your bra, my dear!" Mummy quipped and the others laughed, but I didn't find it funny.

There were other such discussions when we visited, which we were required to, every Sunday I wasn't working. When the subject of child-rearing came up (which it did often, as Rupert's siblings had broods of infants) I said I didn't want to have children. Again, there was a lack of understanding, they couldn't respect any view which didn't sit nicely in middle England. I couldn't stand it. The talk became more heated, but I refused to be a silent wife. They thought Rupert should keep me quiet. They generally spoke to him, not me, and they never learned to pronounce my name correctly.

About the time I became head chef at the hotel, things had got to the point where I realised my marriage was over. Rupert and I had very little in common and didn't share any dreams of a future together, so I left him and his family and their expectations. I found a place to rent near work. It was just a room, as I couldn't afford anything else on my salary, but as I ate all my meals at the hotel and only went there to sleep, it was fine. Rupert didn't come after me — I think he was relieved to see me go — and he was quite reasonable when the divorce discussions began.

When I look back on that time, it's painful to remember, but not because of losing my husband, who had never been a soulmate. It was around that time that my father was first diagnosed with cancer and six months later he was dead. My healthy, supportive, diligent and lovely dad got a horrible type of lymphoma and none of his medical friends or colleagues could save him. I still can't believe it happened and those months are such a blur. I don't know how I came through them, but I did, we all did.

When it was over, my mother decided she was going to go back to Sri Lanka, probably for good. My sister was training to be a surgeon in a northern teaching hospital and had married another doctor, who was everything my husband had not been. I felt so alone. Even my work could not fill the huge gap left after my dad died, so I decided to leave, to go to the other side of the world and start again. I travelled via Sri Lanka, accompanying my mother to her new life en route to mine. We spent a few weeks together at our family house and cooked in my grandmother's kitchen, although by now Ammamma was long gone. Mum and I found her recipes, pencilled in plain notebooks — there were no celebrity cookbooks with glossy photos in my grandmother's day. This brought us closer to her. It helped me to think that Dad was with her now, wherever the dead go. And I developed some new recipes. I enjoyed fiddling with Ammamma's spice mixes (she wouldn't have minded) and creating some more Western adaptations of Eastern dishes. I cooked for my family in Sri Lanka: my aunties, uncles and cousins all came round and they teased me about being the big famous London chef, so did I now think I could tell them how to cook? I wouldn't dare! As I said, Sri Lankan women are strong.

* * *

So that's how I came to be here, in this hospital at the bottom of the world. I have come a long way, from Sri Lanka to the UK and then all the way here to Aotearoa. From a child at my grandmother's knees, to an English wife, to an Antipodean divorcee. From a student of nutrition, to hotel chef and now a hospital catering services manager. While I don't actually prepare much food at work these days, I am still a cook. I know how to feed people properly and I've learned how important that is in hospitals. Research has shown that patients become malnourished within 24 hours of admission: it's called progressing towards a starvation state, because the body starts breaking down its own muscles. When we're designing our menus for patients, I explain to my staff that there are a lot of things to consider. In addition to the usual dietary needs and preferences, there are complicated issues, such as whether the alimentary tract is working properly after surgery, and more obvious things — like whether the patient has teeth to chew with.

I often repeat my mantra when we are at work in our noisy, steamy kitchens:

"We have to feed them well!"

"Yes, Chef!" they yell back. This is one of our in-jokes, because you wouldn't normally be this formal in a hospital kitchen, but I've always set my standards high. I ask my staff to consider why we wouldn't make our best food for those who are sick, to help heal those who need it most. The answer to that question may seem obvious — why wouldn't we? — but it's actually quite complex. It's more a question of why can't we, with our limited budgets, dilapidated equipment which often breaks down, and staff who are expected to do so much for their minimum wage. I ask a lot of questions at work, which doesn't always go down well with my fellow managers, but my Ammamma always taught me to ask if I didn't understand.

And here is something else to consider: cooking is an act of love, an act of caring for someone else. My grandmother taught me this, my mother knew it (oh, the way my father looked at her when she brought her creations to our table!) and I came to know it when I cooked for Suzie back in our university days. It took me many years to understand that loving and caring doesn't always have to be an intimate thing in a private place — we can be that person at work. I love directing the cooking for the patients and staff in this sometimes anonymous-feeling place. The hospital kitchens are huge — we can cook one hundred eggs in a single machine — and really busy, but our food is prepared with care, with each person in mind, with consideration for what each person needs. I don't just hide in the kitchens either: I like to go out and about around the hospital, checking the ward fridges and the fruit bowls I've introduced to give patients access to healthy food when they need it.

The fact that there is a lot to consider is sadly lost on the senior management of this hospital, who are having discussions with external contractors, who say they can provide our food at a cheaper price. They want to cook our hospital's food at a factory hundreds of miles away, then freeze it and transport it in little packages for us to defrost and pour onto patients' plates. Pools of greyness. To me, it's déjà vu — this terrible trend I've seen on the other side of the world, where decent hospital canteens have been replaced by fast food outlets. Lessons have not been learned and the plan for our hospital is completely crazy. I'm sure no cook or nutritionist has been anywhere near it and I'm opposing it with all my might. I sit on various committees and attend these meetings in my chef's whites, which I wouldn't usually wear outside the kitchens, but I think it makes a point. My former in-laws would call me a socialist now. Feminist! Socialist! Me? I am just a cook.

We also make all the food for the staff canteen here on site and I have become known to some as the Goddess of Curries, because they feature regularly on my menus. I get on well with most of the hospital staff and I try to see past the racism which I've come to learn is endemic in the Kiwi workforce. Yes, sadly it is still here. I was the Paki girl in northern England and now I'm the Indian lady in southern New Zealand. Some people can't see past my brown skin. They won't listen when I tell them where I'm actually from, but sometimes my food can speak for me. Even some of the meat-and-two-veg-demanding-roast-lamb traditionalists (I try not to call them racists) change their minds once they have tried my curries. But I'm careful to keep the dishes mild — they don't like too much chilli in the deep south!

I get on especially well with the young doctors in our hospital, perhaps because we understand what it is like to work such long hours, how it feels to have to carry on working when your body is crying out for rest. Recently a couple of them asked me if I would cater for the annual doctors' dinner. We have quite a formal set-up here — the doctors have a room in the basement where they can go to relax and we provide afternoon tea every day. It sounds old-fashioned, I know, but we make neatly cut sandwiches and sliced fruit and pretty cakes — which my team like making as there is more scope for experimenting on the staff — and we serve it from a trolley in the doctors' mess at

3 p.m. on weekday afternoons. There is often a small crowd there, including a few medical students enjoying a cheeky snack at their seniors' expense. The doctors pay a mess fee, but they don't seem to mind sharing their tea with their students. I sometimes pop in on them around this time, to check they're all happy with my food.

One day last week, one of the anaesthetists — a lovely guy called Anil — asked if I would consider doing the food for the doctors' annual dinner.

"The junior doctors want to support the hospital kitchen staff in light of recent threats to outsource our cooking," he explained rather formally.

"Thank you, Anil." I was touched that they had thought to ask this, and suddenly had to blink back tears.

"Also, we all love your curries!" he laughed.

"I'm sure we can do something," I mumbled, trying to regain my composure.

Before I could say any more, another doctor, Matt Williams — who I know from one of my committees — came over to join us. My friend Lizzie, who's now a house officer on E8, was with him. She's always with Matt when I see her these days, but she tells me it's purely professional. Lizzie looks much happier than she was after the selfish surfer dumped her, which is good to see, although she always looks exhausted. She has that junior doctor ghost-look.

"Have you asked her, Anil?" Matt said, as Lizzie nodded hopefully at me.

"He has." I was able to smile now. "And I'm sure I'll soon be able to confirm it will be fine. I'll just tell senior management we are doing it. So which curries would you like?"

We all laughed and Matt and Lizzie hugged me in a sort of scrum, which I've seen on the sports fields around town. They were probably tired and over-emotional — the permanent state of many of us who work here — but we know what it means for our hospital.

It will be a wonderful night. We will decorate the doctors' mess to remove all signs of sickness, of institutional blandness and deterioration. We will cover the cracking walls with fairy-lights and the plastic tables with linen tablecloths, and with plenty of candles we will create another world in our hospital basement for one evening. The managers won't be invited and there will be speeches from those who are loved among us.

And I will cook. I will plan a menu featuring Kiwi adaptations of Eastern recipes. I will use local ingredients — deep burgundy beetroot and golden kumara and beautiful British Racing Green silverbeet — and transform them with magical Sri Lankan spices into dishes fit for kings and queens and all who sail this magnificent hospital ship. The Sunday supplements would call it inspired, but I will just say it's a feast prepared with love. I won't say that to my staff, though. They would tease me as I yelled out my instructions in our hectic kitchen — someone would call it a love-feast and someone else would be sure to mention the *Kama Sutra*. There would be comments about young doctors being horny enough already! We would all laugh as we cooked.

We will laugh anyway: we will talk and joke and gossip, as we wash and chop and create and prepare to serve. We will ignore the poor conditions and try to forget the current threats to our jobs, to our patients' wellbeing, to our lives in this community. For one more evening I will cook and they will eat and they will eat well.

~

The Professor's Tale

She fell in love with him in Buenos Aires. It was complicated, because he wasn't in that famous South American city at the time and the realisation that she was in love took Sarah by surprise. She had travelled there to attend an international conference on women's health and the night before her plenary lecture ('Maximising the safety of therapeutic abortion methods') she had lain awake in her hotel bed sending texts to her friend Anil Malik, who worked at the same hospital, deep in the south of Aotearoa, where she had recently been appointed as Chair of the Department of Obstetrics and Gynaecology.

Sarah knew Anil well because they worked together at least once a week, most often on a Friday morning when she was the surgeon performing the termination of pregnancy list in the day surgery unit. It was not a list she enjoyed, in fact it was harrowing, because she knew most of the women from seeing them in clinic a week or so earlier. She had heard their stories and felt their pain and even after years of doing this work, she still felt their grief and guilt and all the other emotions women feel when having to make one of the hardest decisions of their lives. The men were almost never there — neither at the clinic, nor when their partners lay alone on the trolley waiting to be wheeled into the anaesthetic room. Sarah made a point of greeting each woman as she lay in the anteroom and it was there she noticed Anil's kind and gentle manner, how he put a hand on their arm as he explained the process, how he sent them to sleep with care.

Therapeutic abortion is a relatively simple operation compared with other gynaecological procedures, but there are real risks that require the skill of an experienced surgeon. Sarah taught students and junior colleagues about the TOP procedure, often in theatre while performing the operation herself. She taught them that the pregnant uterus is softer and more easily perforated than when non-pregnant, so care must be taken when dilating the cervix — too much pressure and the metal dilator can easily slip too far into the uterine wall and through to the pelvic cavity. A hole in the pregnant uterus bleeds profusely, and this is already a bloody procedure. The surgeon watches the blood and tissue travel down the clear plastic tube which is part of the evacuation equipment; she watches the receptacle fill. The surgeon notes the blood loss and comes to know when the uterus is empty, when the job is done. She also learns how to become emotionally detached, so she can continue to do this work.

Some of Sarah's colleagues refused to perform thera-peutic abortions, for religious or ethical reasons. This meant more work for her, as the list was always full, but she never challenged their beliefs and they never questioned hers. She wondered if they knew how hard it was for her, especially when — years ago now — she had become pregnant herself and had babies of her own. Privately, Sarah thought that citing religion was an easy escape from the difficulties of conducting abortions. She wondered how the religious objectors thought the other theatre staff dealt with their beliefs — there were a range of people from Christian obstetricians to Muslim porters who helped these women and didn't judge.

One day, during their break in the theatre tearoom, Sarah asked Anil if he was religious.

"Not really. My parents were Hindus, but I never really believed." He dunked a biscuit into his tea and felt the stir of interest their conversations always induced in him. "I'm not sure I have any fixed beliefs these days. Maybe I'm an atheist."

"Even atheists have beliefs." You can't be a man without beliefs, she thought. "And what do you mean by 'fixed'?"

Her eyes started to shine and he noticed her questions had attracted the interest of others — Mary, Dave and two medical students came over to join them. Anil thought it wonderful that she could raise such subjects in her fearless way in the theatre tearoom between cases. He wanted to explain that he did have beliefs — although he didn't agree with organised religion — but not in front of this crowd. He had realised then that he wanted her to himself.

Sarah was someone who got the job done and was competent enough to have become the first female professor of women's health in their region. Anil knew something of what this had involved, because they had both come up through this same hospital as junior doctors and both knew the various characters who played their part in the drama of life in a teaching hospital. There were the old gynae boys who wore three-piece suits and called their patients 'dear', but some of whom — like Mr Rawlinson — had encouraged their junior female colleagues, knowing it was time for women to have a place in their specialty. The orthopods were always the butt of jokes made by the more academic doctors (like Anil and Sarah) but they were friendly enough in the theatre tearoom, especially when the talk was about the latest game, which it often was. When the game was cricket, Anil was on home ground, although he had also played rugby at school (at the English school where the game was invented in fact, but he didn't tell anyone that). Sarah declared both games were macho rituals and refused to join in. Then there were the general surgeons, who looked down on all surgery involving the female pelvis and one of whom had, during a long and complicated abdominal procedure, told Sarah to get out of surgery while she was still a nice girl. Anil had been the gas man on that occasion and had laughed out loud, asking the surgeon what made him think Sarah was nice. Afterwards, he said privately that the dickhead probably fancied her and didn't know how to ask a woman out.

Then there was Mrs Whippy, the theatre sister so named because, instead of the usual blue disposable hat worn by other theatre staff, she wore a white cloth wound around and up onto her head, which looked like the soft swirl ice cream. Anil and Sarah sometimes discussed whether Mrs Whippy knew her nickname. This was how everyone referred to her, but only behind her back — she was too scary to risk it in front of her. Although they joked about her, Mrs Whippy was a vicious woman who liked no one, and whom no one liked. She was particularly nasty to any female surgeons she had the pleasure of intimidating. Sarah recalled how sweat had trickled down her back for hours when she was learning how to do a hysterectomy, with Mrs Whippy making snide comments and telling Sarah — in front of lovely Mr Rawlinson who was calmly taking her through the procedure — not to snatch the instruments. Now that Sarah was the teacher, she still remembered that fear and how at times it had almost stopped her in her tracks.

Anil was a teacher too, now that he was a senior registrar on the anaesthetic rotation. It was a part of the job he enjoyed. He liked to see how the more anxious med students relaxed when he told them they would "see one, do one, teach one!" (the procedures they were trying to learn) and how he could reassure the new house officers about resus, teach them their ABCs, give them tricks of his trade. Now that he'd been around for a few years, he could also help overseas doctors become Kiwi doctors (coming from Mumbai, he knew all about that) and support the hospital kitchen staff in trying to keep their jobs. Anil had earned the privilege of being the go-to man. He found himself hoping that Sarah would ask him to help her in some way, although that was unlikely. He'd never met anyone as independent as Professor Sarah White.

The week before Sarah left for Buenos Aires she was stressed, even more so than usual. There were only five days until her departure and much to be done before she left. Her clinical load had to be reorganised and she needed to find someone to cover her on-call; she had to make arrangements for her teenagers while she was away — her ex-husband was being his usual unhelpful self — and work out who was going to feed the fish and call her mother. There were her teaching commitments too: as the new prof she was still having to prove herself (even if she became Superwoman herself, there would still be critics) and her colleagues weren't falling over themselves to offer support. And then there was the conference — the small matter of her keynote presentation, her first plenary lecture to an international audience. That was something else she would have to keep to herself for now.

At the end of a long and difficult list, not helped by Mrs Whippy's comments about professors going away to too many conferences, Sarah found herself drained and on the point of tears. Anil, who noticed what others hadn't, took her to have a cup of tea in the Atrium café, which offered a *Bistro Environment in the Heart of our Hospital*. It was slightly more private than the staff canteen or the doctors' mess, but the food was pricey and it closed at 5 p.m. when the managers went home.

They found a table in the corner which looked out on the street. Not for the first time, Sarah thought how odd it was that the normal world outside could be so physically close. Time spent in hospitals was so far removed from real life. She watched as it started to rain and shoppers pulled coats around themselves, hurrying home. Anil poured the tea in his usual careful manner — the ritual seemed important to him and Sarah fleetingly wondered again about his religion and heritage, but she wasn't in the mood to discuss that now. He tried to break her anxious silence with an offer of help.

"I could take your fifth years next week. We could do obstetric anaesthesia."

"Thanks, Anil." She still looked tense, so he tried to make her laugh.

"If I can't change my shifts, I could get them to help me with some epidurals on Labour Ward."

She didn't even smile at that one, so he tried again.

"You could look on your trip as a sort of mini-break: no kids, no men, no daughterly duties. Never mind the international meeting! Let's look up if the hotel has a spa or pool."

Sarah tried to cheer up, but couldn't. He knew she minded about everything to do with this conference. Lecturing about therapeutic abortion in a country where the procedure was not legally available was brave.

"I'm scared, Anil." She looked down at her tea as she said this, anywhere so as not to meet his eyes. Sarah was not used to admitting feelings to colleagues — or even to friends — and while Anil suspected this, he only said "Well, I can understand that."

He could imagine the fear of being in a foreign city with your professional reputation on the line. He also knew what it was like to be alone, with no one to hold your hand in the early hours of a sleepless night.

* * *

So now she lay in the middle of such a sleepless night in Buenos Aires, sending Anil text messages as he had instructed her to do any time she felt frightened, or even when she didn't.

"Text any time!" he had said, "My phone is always with me! I'm a text addict, ha ha!" This wasn't true, but he hoped she'd like his joke.

They had been exchanging texts since she left for the airport two days ago — factual messages at first — work stuff, flight information; then some gossip — certain texts featured Mrs Whippy, who had been mysteriously absent from work the day after Sarah left; and then more personal messages as the distances and time zones widened. By the time she arrived in Buenos Aires he had told her he was missing her and had felt distracted and unsettled since she left. She replied that she had found herself thinking a lot about him too, especially during the endless hours over the Pacific Ocean, but, trying to keep some professional context to their relationship, added that she needed to focus on her keynote address which was still unfinished. He replied that she would shine like a star at the conference (he surprised himself that he could be so poetic) and he had no doubt she would excel and impress.

In his mind's eye he could see her on the podium, her copper hair catching the light of the spotlight and her eyes bright with the passion she had for her work. How could they not love her? How could *he* not love her? That second and rather revealing thought came to him during a long orthopaedic case (difficult for the surgeons, but not for him) but he didn't text it, thinking he shouldn't complicate her life. Anil didn't have much experience of love, but he thought it must be very complicated. Also, he was unsure how to diagnose it: what are the symptoms of love? Later, he typed some words into his phone: 'continually distracted', 'obsessively thinking about someone', 'can't concentrate', 'no appetite for food', 'unable to sleep', 'tearful at times', but Dr Google was no help — just as he'd always told the students.

Sarah didn't diagnose it either, until she found herself sending him a text at 3.15 a.m. Buenos Aires time, saying it was a warm night over there and she was lying in her hotel bed, covered only by a sheet. "Wow that just flipped", he texted back — immediately, of course; it was still early evening in Aotearoa — unsure how to respond, but then realising he wanted to be there to touch her, to declare his love in all its complicated forms — it had not felt physical until now. The texting continued until 5 a.m., by which time they had each tentatively admitted it was possible they were in love. At dawn, Sarah put down her phone and began to get ready. As she showered, she thought about how it had already been a big day and wondered again when days and nights and other gestations really began and ended. The hospital — their hospital — in its own time zone, was a world away, but it was with her and within her in so many ways.

Energised and empowered by the emotions of the night, she delivered the best lecture of her life — or at least that's how it felt. She finally understood what it meant to hold an audience in your hands, and afterwards there was genuine interest and thoughtful questions from eminent colleagues. Later that day, during the lunch break, several delegates told her how much they had appreciated her presentation. She became engaged in discussions about potential international collaborations and it felt great to be at the centre of her professional world.

The day ended in the same way it had begun — back in her hotel room with Anil. Kicking off her shoes and raiding the mini bar for a glass of Argentinian wine, she sank into an overstuffed chair. Maybe this was better than being at home. She put on the luxury bathrobe and decided to email Anil about everything. Texts were not enough, she needed to tell him more. Her letter was so obsessively detailed she feared a bored response, but it was met with an even more detailed email describing his thoughts on her day and some notes about his. They shared their observations and interactions: who they had met — new people for Sarah, the usual cast of characters for Anil; what they had eaten — not much for either — and both confessing that thoughts of the other had been omnipresent. Their exchanges deepened in intensity as the night wore on and then at about 3 a.m. (again) he asked her what they should do next. She replied that she just wanted to be with him. He wanted the same: he ached to be with her.

It seemed simple, but it wasn't. Sarah wanted to rush back from Buenos Aires into Anil's arms — for the first time in her life she had fantasies about romantic reunions at crowded airport gates — but that was not going to work for them. As she prepared to leave for the long haul home, they discussed the question of where to meet. Not at the airport: there were bound to be members of the hospital hierarchy sitting in the flight club lounges, on their way to and from various management away-days. Not at her house, where her teenagers slouched behind their screens but noted her every move. Not at Anil's flat: he didn't want her to see the unpacked boxes of books and other signs that it wasn't his home, although he had lived there for two years. He didn't explain why, in his forties, he still felt homeless, but hoped he would be able to tell her all about that soon. For the first time in his life, Anil yearned to share everything with someone else.

The weather in southern Aotearoa had turned wintery since Sarah left, so Anil suggested meeting somewhere warm and private. Neutral territory too, although neither of them used these words. After a few more texts, they booked a suite at a hotel just outside town, some distance from the hospital and a place where generally only tourists could afford to stay. He started to make plans, which of course had to take into account his shifts for that week, but having someone to make plans with was wonderful.

Sarah's journey home felt like a lifetime: for those hours when they could not be in immediate contact, there was no point to anything. There was just the waiting to be together. She wanted to tell someone she was in love. She needed to explain how she felt, how she had been thrown from her horse and couldn't get up; ask someone who had been in love, what it had felt like. But there was no one to ask or tell: the woman in the seat next to her had been snoring for hours. Sarah retrieved her laptop and started another letter to Anil. She wrote and wrote as the plane roared through another night without sleep. At an unknown hour, it occurred to her that she might have made all of this up, dreamt it during the altered time zones of South America, and that she had somehow created another consciousness. Perhaps normality would be restored as she re-entered her native time and place. When she arrived at the hotel perhaps he would say it had all been a joke. Maybe they would laugh nervously and go their own ways back to the hospital, or to their respective houses. Maybe seeing her kids again would wake her up to the fact she was in fact a middle-aged mother, not a love-sick adolescent. And perhaps going back to work would remind her she was a professor of O&G, not a South American goddess.

* * *

They met at the hotel the day after her return. Sarah's teenagers were still asleep, oblivious in their Sunday morning lie-in, so she took time choosing her clothes — a soft wrap-around dress, boots with a sexy heel — and applying some make-up, hopefully to hide the bags under her eyes. She drove towards their rendezvous, taking back streets and parking around the corner on a side road. Anil met her in the parking lot and she kissed him on the cheek. He was awkward, but as they went up to the room together he took her hand. It felt warm and small in his. Anil suddenly thought about how Mrs Whippy used to complain that she had to order extra-small gloves for Sarah. He must tell her more about the theatre sister's disappearance, although no one knew much about it. But he didn't want to talk about that now, there were more important things to discuss.

Sarah was still tired from her journey and for some time they sat drinking tea at a low table by the window. It was not

[110]

as luxurious as the hotel in South America (no over-stuffed chairs) but it felt more like home. Anil had bought her fair trade tea and some expensive gourmet biscuits, which they nibbled on, instead of the stale-looking offerings in the hotel's hospitality basket. When she opened the fridge to look for some water, she noticed a bottle of champagne and some exquisitely wrapped chocolate bars. The sight of those items affected her — that he would think to do that.

They talked about the conference, her travels, the hospital. After a while they became quiet and Sarah noticed the trees outside the window. In the short time she had been away, the exotics had lost their leaves, but the ngaio were still glossy and the kowhai offered sprays of foliage, tiny green bouquets. She was happy to be home. She told Anil she hadn't liked what she had seen of Buenos Aires, the slums on the way from the airport, the cracked pavements. The taxi driver had told her that children could only go to school in the morning or afternoon, not both, as the state couldn't afford it. Anil sighed gently and took her hand again. It was a beautiful hand. She took his hand as they sat at the table: both hands touching, four hands entwined.

Later that afternoon they made love on the hotel bed. Sarah found herself naked in the fading light of that winter afternoon, being kissed from fingers to neck, from toes to thighs, breasts to lips. He was tantalisingly slow in his attention to detail and she shuddered violently at the point of orgasm, which came early and urgently. She wept with its release and afterwards he held her in his arms, stroking her hair, kissing her face. He called her my love, and she cried some more as he held her close, their heads touching, bodies interlaced. There was then a stillness, an emptiness which became filled with the most intense connection she had ever known, a closeness beyond physical love.

When it became dark, he thought about fetching the champagne from the fridge, asking if she would like some food from room service, or suggesting they go to the hotel restaurant. But he didn't want to move, or be somewhere he couldn't feel and touch the entirety of her. She lay across him now and he stroked her hair and back. He wanted to map her skin out again and again with his fingers, to know every intimate place. Yet it was already enough. As Sarah's head became heavier on his shoulder, he thought of how he had read about moments of complete fulfilment, but never understood. Now he knew. He had called her his love and they both realised what that meant. He wanted to make love again and again, but he also felt calm, that future explorations could wait.

As Sarah dozed quietly in his arms, Anil thought about the privilege of being with someone as they slept. He had spent his career putting people to sleep, but he had never slept a night — or even a few hours — with anyone in this way. As a younger man he had been more than ready to go back to his flat alone after sexual encounters with other women. Sleeping with someone: what we say when we mean we're having sex with another, but sleep is often not part of that. To Anil, sleeping with another person felt more intimate than sex. Sarah, his friend and now his lover, had trusted him with such intimacy and it moved him. Her breathing now told him she was sound asleep and he felt a strong protectiveness as he drew the covers around them.

He kissed the top of her head, inhaling her smell. Gently pushing back curls from the side of her face, he kissed her temple. She smiled in her sleep. He had never seen her so relaxed, never felt her like this before, and he thought maybe he had given her something after all.

Anil found himself thinking back to their Friday mornings together in theatre, those heart-breaking sessions working their way through the TOP list. She was always so professional. He was too, although he knew he was merely an observer. Or perhaps 'assistant' was a better term, as he couldn't just stand by and watch. He did what he could. It must have hurt her, ending those grains of life which didn't grow any further. She was a mother, after all. He thought about tissue travelling down plastic tubes, some of it to be labelled 'products of conception' and studied under microscopes by pathologists in the labs off the back corridors of their hospital. Possibilities which had not become realities.

Anil realised he had only come to know Sarah today. The possibility of love had become their reality: that undefinable, unsettling thing, already growing between them, had been given new life when she left for Buenos Aires. Her departure had captured him, and when she came back, he had captured her. So here they were together.

She opened her eyes and touched his face. In the light from the bedside clock, she could see he was smiling. It was 10.25 p.m. and he asked her quietly if she had to go home, back to her kids.

"No, I don't. It's all sorted. Arrangements have been made. Believe it or not, my mother is helping me out."

He laughed quietly and said "Well, well." Anil knew all about Sarah's mother.

"How about you? Can you stay the night with me?"

"Yes, please." He was grinning, but felt like crying too.

~

The Night Nurse's Tale

~ ROSIE ~

My working day starts at ten at night, when my shift on ward E8 begins. I've been working nights for years, and most of them on this same ward, imaginatively named after the corner of the floor of this now elderly building. When I first qualified as a nurse, this hospital was brand spanking new and we were all excited to get jobs here. I'd done my training at the old hospital in the centre of town, which had Nightingale wards where the beds were so close together the patients could have held hands if they had wanted to. They didn't, of course, because they were too old and too sick, but the more alert ones did sometimes talk to each other. Nowadays it's much harder for the patients to chat, as the six beds in each bay are well separated and every bed has its own TV set. A lot of my patients spend their stay in hospital plugged into that box all day, so when I arrive for my shift I try to get them to disconnect and talk with me for a while.

I usually arrive about 9.30 p.m., which gives me time to get myself sorted before I start my shift. Coming into the hospital through the main entrance, it's generally pretty quiet by that time, especially on a Sunday evening. During the week, Raelene sometimes leaves me a note which I collect from Reception on my way in: it's an old habit we've kept up through all the years we've worked together, and although we more often text these days, we still find it amusing to leave each other messages in the brown envelopes marked CONFIDENTIAL. There's no envelope for me tonight, but Tipene the night porter is keen to chat.

"How are you this evening, Rosie? Having a good weekend?"

He beams at me, shuffling the weight between his feet. This signals he's got things to tell me. Tip is always full of tales — which my mother would call tittle-tattle — about various members of staff. Last Monday he intercepted me on my way up to the ward.

"Did you hear that Raelene's found herself a fancy-man?"

I'd heard all about that months ago (some of it via the brown envelopes) and it wasn't news to me, but I just said, "Lucky her!" and smiled as I went on my way. I was running late as I'd needed to drop off a prescription for Dad before coming into work.

On Tuesday, Tip had more gossip he wanted to share. He caught me in Reception again, as I'd stopped to talk to Lizzie, the house officer on our ward who's on nights this week. She and Matt were on their way through Reception to A&E, to see who they might have for us. Tip came over to tell us all that Raelene's affair had been going on for some time and the guy was a foreigner, maybe an Arab, who had come to work in our hospital.

"Maybe he's got a magic carpet and will take her away to distant lands!" I said dramatically, rolling my eyes at Lizzie.

"I wish my life was anywhere near as exciting," I continued, before Tip could start up again.

"I've come to think excitement is a bit over-rated," Lizzie said, a bit wistfully. She looked tired.

Matt yawned. "Yeah, I'm hoping for a really boring night tonight."

"I'll do my best, kiddies," I called after them, as they went on their way and I headed towards the lifts and up to the ward.

On Wednesday evening, Tip was unusually quiet when I came into work. I asked how his day had been.

"Not bad," he said. "I hear it's been busy on Delivery Suite this week."

"At least that's something you and me don't have to worry about any more!" I chuckled. Tip nodded but didn't shuffle his feet.

Tonight, he's more his usual self again. I reply to his enquiry about my weekend with "Good, thanks." Kiwi-speak for we don't really want to talk about it.

Tip is undeterred. "What time's your break?"

"Probably the usual, why?"

"More news to tell you! Exciting stuff!" he taps the side of his nose like a character in a bad sitcom. I'm not really in the mood for Tip this evening, it's been a long week, and his 'news' is probably just more silly stuff about Raelene and Mohammed. However, I tell him I'll catch him later and leave him to pounce on the next member of staff lumbering into the hospital for another night of fun.

Up on E8 I make for the changing room. I come to work in my uniform, which I tell people is because it's easier to change at home, but it's also because I am morbidly obese and don't want any of my colleagues to see me without clothes on. That harsh and confronting description of my size was used by a slip of a girl — who I suspected had an eating disorder — as she weighed me during a workplace health check. She was smug and condescending as she put my height and weight into her shiny computer and told me the result. Then she labelled me. I would have just said I was too fat. I know I'm overweight and that's how people see me — Rosie the fat night nurse — but there's more to me than my body. People also refer to me as the cheerful one, because I laugh a lot and sometimes I tell jokes, even on the drug round. You need a sense of humour in this job.

My ward is general medical, which back in the day would have been called geriatrics. The patients are old and often dying: they are crumbling like our hospital, which we are now told has leaky building syndrome. I was chatting about this with one of my lovely old men last week as I was cleaning him up after an especially messy faecal accident. There was shit everywhere — running down his legs, in the bed, on the floor, on my shoes — and it's good to have something to talk about during these massive clean-up operations. I'm used to it, but you have to remember that they are not, and people still feel embarrassment and pride in old age. So I nattered on and he quipped that he had 'leaky person syndrome' because he is now doubly incontinent. We laughed at his joke behind the thin curtains which are all that protect our patients from the stares of others. Hospital curtains! I tell the students and junior docs to remember you can hear everything through those curtains, even if you can't see everything. You only have to be a patient for one night on a hospital ward to hear life and death going on behind those billowing strips of standard-issue material. The young ones look at me strangely when I tell them that — they are new to all this, so healthy (so thin) and the only nights they have spent in hospital have been on the right side of those curtains. They're all so clever too — even the nursing students have degrees now, which we didn't need. I have hardly any qualifications, just my nursing certificate and the time I've spent looking after the sick.

I have a sort of ritual each evening after I arrive on the ward. First, in the changing room I take off my coat, pin on my badge, then my nurse's watch and check it is working properly. I've only ever had one watch — my parents bought it for me when I got into nursing school and it's never let me down. I keep it in its original box and only pin it on when I get to work, so that I don't lose it or throw it into the laundry by mistake. Then I check I have what I need in my pockets, including a pen that actually works. After that, I tidy my hair in the mirror and put on some lipstick — not a bright gaudy colour of course (my old nursing tutors would never have allowed that) but something cheerful. I like my patients to see me smart and professional, but also happy. Who wants to see a miserable nurse when you've been lying in bed ill all day?

Sometimes I don't feel that happy, though. I've been having trouble with my periods lately. I went to see my GP, who told me I had 'flooding', when I told her that each month my blood flowed through layers of tampons and pads and sometimes soaked my clothes with its dark stain.

Those days have to be planned around toilets, without telling anyone why, without explaining why I am tired and worried about what people might see. My doctor sent me to see Prof White in our gynae department, who was sympathetic — better than the old gynae boys used to be — but she's young and pretty, and very slim. She asked if I could lose some weight, as this was undoubtedly contributing to the heaviness of my periods. I said I would try and went away feeling miserable and longing for menopause.

Once I've done my lipstick, I go out onto the ward and make a quick round of the patients to say hello and see who's still with us since my last shift. I don't mean to see who has died, because people do get better and go home too, even from our ward, and these days more often than before. Back in the Nightingale ward days, patients were sometimes with us for months, but now they are moved to rehabilitation units or other care facilities, which do what we used to do, but probably better and with more qualifications.

I'm not meant to visit my patients until after hand-over, but I like to check in with them before I hear the official report of their day. Before I speak to them, their faces tell me what sort of a day they've had, if they are in pain, if they are getting better. Usually they are pleased to see me, especially the ones who recognise me from the night before. They like to tell me how they are, who has visited them (and who hasn't) and what they've been watching on telly, although often they can't remember. Later I'll return to each of them to help them get settled for sleep, do my nursing duties to help them through their nights.

Sometimes people ask me why I've always worked nights. Depending on who's asking, I might say it was good when the kids were younger, as I would be home in time for breakfast and to take them to school. Then I could sleep during their day, pick them up and have the early evening with them. I loved being with Jimmy and Helen — they were great kids and those after-school evenings of mealtimes and homework around our kitchen table were the core of our family life. My husband John is in the police and most of the time we could arrange things so we all had tea together. Then, once the kids were in bed, I would go off to work at the hospital and my working day would begin.

So it suited my family arrangements in those days and I just carried on. If a close friend, like Raelene, asked me why I didn't change my night shifts after the kids left home, I might confide that it's because I don't want to sleep with John any more. He snores and writhes around all night and I prefer to sleep on my own these days. I might joke that he is now old and fat and so am I, and we don't fancy each other any longer, but this is only partly true. John still fancies me, still wants to have sex with me all the time. He adores me and my body as much as he did twenty years ago, but I don't feel the same. When he gets a chance, he still wants to penetrate me: he pulls out his dick and expects me to stroke it and suck it and worship it before he thrusts it into me. But I can't — especially if it's when I am doing the dishes after tea, or trying to read a book in bed. It's not just that I'm never in the mood these days — his body repulses me: it's too much, it's too suddenly produced. I can't seem to respond to him or his dick any more. Maybe a therapist would say it's because I don't love my own body, or that I don't love John any more. Neither of these things is true. I still love my fat and dysfunctional body with all its flaws. And I still love John — he may be a bit ugly and have no idea about foreplay, but he's a good man and we can still have a laugh together. I wouldn't see a therapist anyway.

When I'm working nights, if I get a quiet moment, I sometimes think about how relationships change over the years, about how our lives change. As I help my patients get comfortable for the night, I talk with them about all sorts of things — they fascinate me. Some of them have been through so much together, making my twenty-five years of relative peace with John seem a bit insignificant. The old folk sometimes chat about their families and I wonder if they miss their spouses as they lie alone in these hospital beds towards the end of their lives. I know that some of them do. One eighty-year old lady who was admitted to our ward after a heart attack told me it was the first time she'd spent a night away from her husband in nearly sixty years. How strange it must have felt for her. Or maybe she was relieved to have time to herself after all these years. It's so hard to get space in a marriage, isn't it? Well, that's how it seems to be for women — our lives are filled with husbands and children and laundry and housework and everything else. For years on end there's never a moment for ourselves. I remember one appointment with my old GP when the kids were younger: I was tired all the time, worried about pretty much everything and feeling really low. Looking after everyone else seemed too much. He asked me if I had any hobbies, anything I liked doing for myself. I laughed out loud and told him hobbies are for men — when on earth would I have time for a hobby? Although he had made me laugh, he didn't look very pleased and churned out a prescription for some anti-depressants and other tablets to help me sleep. I didn't take them, of course.

* * *

After the last drug round of the day and once the patients are settled for sleep, we turn out their lights and the ward becomes a different place. A hospital ward is never completely dark, or totally silent — we have lights on around the nurses' station and there is always the background hum of the building, punctuated by the more acute noises of the numerous machines monitoring or mending our patients. The other nurses spend the rest of the night at our station in a pool of light, reading women's magazines from cover to cover and snacking on food out of packets. I don't do either. The magazines are trying to sell us a life we can't have, bodies we will never have, and they leave me feeling miserable. The packets are also a substitute for real life, for real food. At least we still have proper meals at our hospital, although I hear that they are under threat again.

I normally try to take my break around 2 a.m., when the canteen opens for an hour. By this time, I'm ready to get away from the ward and tonight is no exception. We're completely full after this first week of winter and they're lining them up in A&E. Dan, the charge nurse for our floor, came around earlier to do the nightly bed check.

"There's not a spare bed anywhere tonight," he announced to those of us at the nurses' station. He looked a bit stressed.

[123]

"Don't worry, Dan," I said. "You'll be the first person I call if anyone on E8 karks it tonight".

"Thanks, Rosie." He winked at me as he ran off into the night. I've known Dan for years, but it's only recently I've noticed he's started wearing trainers to work. Maybe he's on some health or fitness programme.

Before leaving for my break, I check the patients are sleeping, or resting as well as they can. If there's someone needing special care, or distressed because they can't sleep, then I won't go. I would rather sit with them until they are calmer, perhaps reading to them quietly once there is no other nursing to be done. The old folk like me reading to them — I have a small collection of books, mostly short stories or poetry (they can't follow anything too long or complicated) that I keep on a table in the day room for anyone to pick up. I don't think they're used much — the patients are plugged into their TVs all day long and the staff are too busy — but I read them at night to those who can't sleep. I speak softly, just loud enough to be heard over the machines. I am not sure how much they take in, as they are often confused or drowsy, but it seems to calm them and they drift back to sleep more quickly than after sleeping pills.

They are all quiet enough tonight, although Mr Black isn't looking too good. I ask Charlie to keep an eye on him as I leave the ward. She looks up from her mag. "Sure. See ya later."

I walk the corridors in my soft-soled flat shoes — some of the doctors wear heels, clicking too loudly above the humming darkness — and weave my way towards the canteen, through the hospital at night. It's a different place without the daytime routines, without the rushing daytime people. The offices and services are closed (not a manager in sight after 5 p.m.) and the wards are shadowy with focuses of light where needed. The building drones to itself as I make my way — it's feeling its age — but even in the dead of night it cannot rest.

The canteen is busy, as usual. People are coming and going. The staff from the wards which never sleep — Delivery Suite, A&E, ICU — don't stay long, rushing away in their scrubs carrying bottles of fizzy drinks to keep their energy levels up. However, there are some like me who can take a short break and it's good to catch up with people from other wards. Sally, who works on the psych unit, always has a few tales to tell. I wouldn't trust her though, any more than I would believe most of Tip's stories.

Tip is here now, holding court at one of the tables in the middle of the canteen. As I queue up to pay for my tea and snack, I can hear him regaling the group with his latest.

"On Thursday, a schizo escaped from psych and was apprehended in main reception when he started singing some bloody opera or something."

"Sounds about right," I hear Sally comment. No one ever seems to question where Tip gets his information. After I've paid, I look over and he waves. There's no escape tonight. Tip calls out, "Rosie, come and join us."

I waddle over and plonk myself down at the far end of the table from Tip, who is now slurping the rest of his tea. I blow gently on mine as he starts up again. He's a nice enough bloke, but he really loves the sound of his own voice.

He goes on for a bit about how the kitchen staff have put themselves up to cater the doctors' dinner this year. Sally makes a comment about how she hopes they like curries, because that's what they'll be getting. Someone else says something else, I'm not sure what, I'm not really listening. I've just about finished my cup of tea when Tip puffs up his chest and offers us his best, his breaking news, which he's been saving till now.

"Did you hear that the new prof is having it away with one of the anaesthetists?" He grins, nodding round at everyone at our table.

"Sarah White?" Sally's eyebrows arch skywards. "I thought she was away this week?"

"That Indian guy?" someone else asks.

Now he has our attention, Tip is full of it, detailing how just yesterday, when he was taking his kids to soccer, he had seen Dr Malik driving out to the airport.

There are a few more questions from the crowd and then Tip asks me what I think of his big news, what I think of Dr Anil Malik.

"Well, it's all a bit of a bugger," I say. "I quite fancied him myself!"

They all laugh. Rosie's hilarious, isn't she? After a bit more chat I excuse myself to go to the loo before going back to work. Once I've sorted myself out (it's that time of the month again) I put on a bit more lipstick and look at myself in the mirror. The face that looks back at me is old and worn out.

I make my way back to E8, hoping that all will be as quiet as when I left. I pass the homeless man who sleeps near one of the back doors. I see him most nights. He always says, "Night, nurse," as I pass by, and now and then I give him a sandwich or some fruit, which I buy for him at the canteen. I don't have anything for him today, but I still say hello. When I get back to the ward, I check in again with Charlie and then go quietly around all the beds, making sure that drips are still running, patients are still sleeping, still breathing. Mr Black looks worse, but he seems comfortable enough. They say the darkest hour is before dawn and it's true, because this is when most of the deaths on our ward seem to happen. Sometimes it's peaceful and sometimes it's not.

Tonight it's not. Mr Black has a cardiac arrest at 4 a.m. on his way to the toilet. I'm helping him walk over there — he was determined not to use a bedpan — and somehow I know it's going to happen. When it does, I do what I can. I call the team and Lizzie, Matt and Michael arrive quickly. They do their stuff, but we all know it's over for Mr Black tonight. After they call time, we carefully lift our patient back onto his bed and I pull the curtains around us. It's just him and me now and I talk quietly as I prepare him. I tell him what I'm doing, what will happen next. We'll keep him with us until I've called his daughter; I'll say that she and her mum can come and see him here, rather than in the mortuary. Dan can wait for the bloody bed! It's what I'd want for my dad, when the time comes.

When I've finished cleaning up Mr Black, I close the curtains behind me and go to visit the other patients in his bay. They're all awake of course, they know what's happened, so I chat to each of them for a while and help them settle back down to rest, if not sleep. It will be getting light soon, so that will help.

My shift ends with hand-over to the day staff. We summarise what sort of night it has been. After we're done, I make my way back to the locker room, go to the toilet again. When I come out, I decide to leave my watch on my dress this morning and put my coat on over the top. I take the lifts down to the ground floor and as I'm walking through Reception I see Raelene just coming into work. It's good to see her, especially after the night I've just had.

"Hiya!" she calls. Raelene always has a smile on her face and these days she has more to grin about than most of us.

"Hi," I say, a bit limply. "You're in early."

"You look worn out!" Raelene chirps as she sets her bag down on the reception desk.

"It's been a bit of a night. A bit of a week really."

"Got time for a coffee? Looks like you need one."

I shouldn't really say yes, because leaving the hospital is not the end of my working day. Every morning, I visit my parents on my way home. They are old now and Dad has dementia, but they still live in their own home, where they've been for fifty years. My mother manages with a determination I don't think I would have to care for John, if he ever becomes incontinent and can't remember who anyone is. She depends on my visit each morning — I bring in shopping and help get Dad out of bed, and make breakfast for the three of us.

But it's only 7 a.m. and Mum doesn't get up until around 8, so perhaps I can go a bit later today. I'll tell them I got held up at work.

"That'd be lovely," I say to Raelene. "Where shall we go?"

"I've gotta be at my desk soon, but we could get one to have here. I'll run and get them from the bistro," and she goes off to ask them to open up a bit earlier than usual. I move around the back of her desk and take her bag and jacket off the counter, putting them underneath, where I know she likes to keep them. I take my coat off, pull up a chair next to hers, on our side of Reception. From where I'm sitting I can see Raelene asking bistro man to fire up his coffee machines. There's some interesting body language going on, but she seems to be winning. I find a scrap of paper and write a short note, which I stuff into one of the envelopes she keeps on her desk. It doesn't say much, just that I hope she and Mohammed will be really happy together. I draw a smiley face, rather than signing my name. She'll know who it's from. I realise that it's the sort of message you'd put in a wedding card and this reminds me to ask her when it will be. Hopefully they'll wait until spring, which would give me time to lose some weight.

Raelene is back with our coffees and we make ourselves comfortable behind her desk, watching all the Monday morning people arriving for their next week of work. We see the night staff leaving; the first patients of the day arriving; theatre staff in their scrubs grabbing a quick coffee before the morning lists begin. Raelene knows almost everyone who works here, but she's not a gossip. In fact, she's so discreet I often have to wrangle information out of her.

"Tip was full of crap last night." I start relating his theories about various members of staff and what they've been up to this week.

"He usually is," Raelene laughs and says she's heard a few things too. We briefly discuss his sighting of Dr Malik and conclude Tip must be wrong about that one.

"But I hope it's true," Raelene says. "They're both so lovely."

"God, you're a romantic softie these days. Maybe they're both just after some casual sex".

"Maybe," she chuckles again. "Who knows?"

"Hopefully they do. The younger generation seem to know what they want, don't they."

This prompts Raelene to ask me how Jimmy and Helen are. I say they are busy with their own lives. I don't need to tell her much more because Raelene knows Jimmy has a good job with the Department of Conservation and Helen's a med student, in her fifth year now, training in Auckland. Suddenly I miss my kids. I haven't seen either of them for ages. I miss coming home from work to wake them up, their fresh young faces, even their grumpy teenage faces. These thoughts quieten me and other heavier ones press in. All the faces which won't wake up again. Like Mr Black today.

A young woman comes up to the desk to ask directions to day surgery. I watch Raelene at work and am comforted by the fact that things go on as usual, even when the worst happens. I try to stop thinking about death, but then I start thinking about my parents. I'd better get going soon, they'll be waiting for me. I'd like to tell Raelene how I dread going to see them every day and how that makes me feel guilty, but she's occupied with other things now, and here's not the place for that sort of chat anyway. Would she understand how the smell of age turns my stomach? Sometimes I have to clean Dad up if he has messed the bed, or didn't get to the toilet in time, and although this is what I do most nights at work, it's not easy when it's your own father. Most days he still seems to know who I am, but I almost wish he didn't when I'm wiping his bum or pulling on the nappies he now wears. I try to chat to Dad, but we can only talk about the present because he can't remember the past — not even five minutes ago — and he can't understand or imagine the future. I've come to thinking this is a good thing, as understanding his future would frighten him. It frightens me. I sometimes wish it would all be over quickly for him, before my mother gets worn into the ground with caring for him, before he needs to go into a dementia unit and leaves her alone in their house, wondering where her life went.

As if she can read my thoughts, Raelene asks, "How's your mum doing? It must be hard for her, with your dad and everything."

"She's okay. Well, she's managing, I guess."

I want to say that we are starting to prepare for my father to die. That I hope it happens somewhere peaceful where he will be cared for as I try to care for my patients every night. I want to tell Raelene that I fear it will still be me who helps wash him, reads to him, tends to him as he slips away. But I don't say any of this, not now. There are more people coming in through the main entrance towards Reception, so I start to gather my things. As I chuck my empty coffee cup into the bin under Raelene's desk, I say, "I'm trying not to think about my old age and who'll care for me when that time comes. It's too depressing! I've told the kids they must shoot me well before I become like Grandad, or the other poor old souls on my ward."

"They don't take me seriously, though. Jimmy just grunts and asks if I'd like to choose which gun he should use from his hunting collection."

Raelene says "Kids!" Then she looks straight at me. "Make sure you tell Helen you want to wear pink lipstick in your coffin."

We both laugh and I feel better. Raelene needs to attend to someone else now. Another Monday morning is cranking up and I'd better go and do my duties at home.

"Thanks for the coffee." I put on my coat to face the sleet outside.

Raelene directs another patient on their way and then, as there is no one else at the desk, she turns to me, opens her arms wide and throws them around me. It must look a bit silly as I'm so huge and she's quite small, but I'm grateful for that hug. I hug her back, then push her away, still holding onto both her arms so I can see her square on.

"It's about time you set a date for your wedding. We all need something to look forward to this winter."

She smiles back and blows a kiss after me as I leave the hospital.

~

Acknowledgements

This is my first work of fiction and I was initially anxious about sharing my stories with anyone. I will be eternally grateful for the early listening, reading and encouragement of my friends Paul Enright, Tharani Sivananthan and George Smerdon. Then the first review of my manuscript by writer friends Rebecca Smith and Peter Winship gave me hope that I could do this. I thank all five of you for helping me over the edge, into this other world.

As the stories accumulated and were formed into a book, other friends and colleagues read drafts. Thanks to Anne Ballinger, Mark Bevin, Fenella Devereux, Jane Hall, Helen Holden, Raewyn Macfie, Yolanda van Heezik, Tracy White, Sue Wootton and Mami Yamaguchi. Later, Dunedin writers Margaret Bell Thomson and Paul Sorrell provided detailed review and feedback. I am very grateful for your diligent and constructive help.

I sought advice on current aspects of hospital practice, and acknowledge Chris Lundy, Helen Paterson and Adam Tiley for their input. Thanks to Anthony Ritchie for providing musical consultation on 'The Cleaner's Tale', and to Tharani Sivananthan and Devonie Waaka for reviewing 'The Cook's Tale' and 'The Obstetrician's Tale' respectively.

Also, thanks to my Medical Humanities peer group in Dunedin, especially Mavis Duncanson, Katherine Hall and Peter Radue, for reading selected stories and providing critical review.

My family has also been supportive of my venture into the world of writing, especially my parents, Jean and Bob Harrison, and my children Alexander and Katharine Woolrych.

Way back when I was at high school in Watford, England, I asked my English teacher if I should be a doctor or a writer. He said I should do both. It's taken me a long time, but I thank Bill Grimwood for all he and my other teachers did for so many of us kids at Queens' School.

My last — and first — thanks are for Jonny. We met as house surgeons in Portsmouth in 1990 and have been together ever since, weaving medical careers with our family life, migration across the world and other interesting journeys. I can't begin to detail all the ways in which Jonny has supported and loved me — there are so many — and for over twenty-five years he has believed that I could write this book.

Dr Mira Harrison
has worked in hospitals, universities and government agencies in Aotearoa and Britain for almost thirty years. Mira followed a career in clinical obstetrics and gynaecology, women's health research and monitoring the safety of medicines. She has written and edited two medical books: *Medicines for Women* and *An Introduction to Pharmacovigilance*.

Since 2001, Mira has lived in Otepoti, Dunedin, Unesco-designated City of Literature, with her husband and two children. She still works in pharmacovigilance and medical ethics, but spends an increasing amount of time writing. *Admissions* is her first work of fiction.